He and Nikonar often spoke of the war that had been raging, a war that most humans were oblivious to. Nor would they care, as miserable as most of their lives were, because at that time in Europe, there were more wolves than humans. That hideous plague which had ridden in on the rats' fleas was killing off the people by the thousands. The vampires' food was being depleted, and wars between them raged nightly as they fought over the few healthy, remaining herds. Villicus assumed Nikonar wanted to again talk about ways to end the war, and he was amused at the location chosen for that night.

SPIRES

By Briar Lee Mitchell

Chapter One

Fire had raged since dawn, a blazing monster that threatened to completely immolate not only the fertilizer factory where it began but also the buildings close by.

Bombs of flame and flying shrapnel, sent airborne by exploding tanks of chemicals, had shattered many of the stained glass windows in the old St. Bartholoma church nearby. Cars and trucks on the streets smoldered helplessly.

The fire department in nearby Stuttgart had dispatched several pumper trucks and firefighters. Shielding themselves from the heat, they moved hoses as closely as possible. The powerful streams of water turned to steam before they could do much good at extinguishing the inferno.

Fire Chief Harald Engel positioned his men around the buildings; the factory was a total loss, so he focused his attention on trying to save the old church. Fire hoses were turned on the thick stone walls, washing them and the roof. Huge strips of aged moss had already ignited, providing a ready, dry source for the flames to consume. Several large pieces tore free from the ancient roof and carried the burning strips to other areas that had not burned yet.

Some local parishioners, passing the barricades erected to keep them out of the danger area, raced in and out of the church. They clutched paintings, sacred relics and all the appointments for the altar as they stumbled and ran through the black smoke fed by the burning chemicals. The factory was not only ablaze; it was roaring, screaming as more and more of the chemical tanks exploded and sent massive columns of flame skyward.

Some of the heavy-duty containers in the factory that

had been designed to hold more volatile chemicals finally finished cooking off and exploded with a deafening boom. The explosions sent out blasts of air that initially extinguished some of the nearest flames and then caught fire themselves, acting like enormous flamethrowers that spread the inferno even further in the vicinity.

Harald, directing his men, hollered into his handheld mic, moving them around the perimeter of the fire like chess pawns. He froze, looking anxiously toward the factory. Every instinct he had told him this was going to be bad.

First, he felt the rumble, then watched in horror as the gigantic building blew up and out, sending thousands of bricks flying like shrapnel and massive metal girders hopping and bouncing like Olympian sized pogo sticks.

People and machines tumbled and flew across the road from the blast. Harald hit the ground, making sure his mask and helmet were securely in place. Bricks rained down all around him and the other firefighters. As quickly as they could, they crawled under the bigger trucks, listening to the projectiles slamming into the vehicles. As far as fires and disasters go, Harald could not remember one worse than this.

Volunteers running from the church with precious relics cradled in their arms now used them to shield their heads from the debris that rained down on them. An elderly woman who was staggering out of the church with a large oil painting of the Virgin Mary hoisted the huge canvas up and over her back as she scuttled past Harald and the other firefighters. Bits of metal and wood pelted the taut canvas, making it sound like a primitive drum. More volunteers raced to the woman's aid, dragging her and the painting to safety.

Another, much bigger, blast from the factory knocked more people off their feet and ignited a nearby tree. The dry fall leaves went up in a flash, turning it into a bonfire resembling a calling of the clans, its massive boughs stretched out like crucified arms. More shrapnel flew into the church, blowing out the few remaining stained glass windows. Bits of colored glass, like deadly gems, spit through the air, cutting people and embedding themselves in tree trunks fifty feet away.

Several large girders, slick with chemicals and ablaze with deadly fire, slammed into the east wall of the sanctuary. Everyone watched, spellbound, as the wall caved, then after a few heartbeats, the entire church folded in on itself like a massive circus tent coming down. The rumble of stones and ancient timbers bouncing off the ground and each other was deafening.

The falling structures created a huge gust of wind that blew tons of ash, shattered glass and dirt in all directions. People either dove for cover behind enormous, ancient trees that swayed treacherously close to snapping or fire trucks that rocked crazily back and forth, flipping gear off the top and from compartments that tore open.

That final blast had all but extinguished the inferno in the factory. The firefighters rushed toward it, dousing the area with water and chemical retardants, killing off the few remaining blazes. Harald crawled out from under the truck where he and others had taken shelter, then ordered his men to stop pouring water on what was left of St. Bartholomas.

He overheard someone in the crowd murmuring that perhaps they could use the stones to shore up the old bridge. Another person bent down and picked up a piece of wood, with one side highly polished from people having walked over it for centuries. They stared at the fragment, as if it were a living, wounded creature, then hugged it to their breast.

St. Bartholoma had stood on this spot for nearly 800 years. It had survived the freezing winters of Germany, Charlemagne's battles, the Ottoman Empire and WWII. After all of that, a fire in a factory that made fertilizer from chemicals and animal dung finally brought it down, reducing it to a ruined heap before them.

Harald turned to the crowd.

"I think it's a total loss," he told them.

He saw a few heads nod and could hear a few people sobbing quietly. Mostly, these people were just exhausted and numb, having risked their own lives to save what they could. He observed the sad little pile of items they had managed to get out of the church. It did not seem like much to him, but a few of the women, moving silently and with great purpose, were already cleaning the soot and dirt off of them.

One woman picked up a heavy chalice and wrapped it reverently in her sweater, then cradled it like it was a small child. He also noticed a priest moving through the crowd, comforting people. Another person who appeared to be in shock shuffled along, looking at the ground. Harald realized the gentleman was picking up bits of glass from the shattered windows, but only the red pieces. Paramedics quickly found him and led him away to be taken to the nearby hospital.

"Father!" Harald called out.

The priest made his way over to the fire chief and extended his hand. Harald shook it.

"You and your men did all that you could," the priest consoled him.

A frightening, groaning sound emanated from the remains of the cathedral. Harald, the priest and the gathered parishioners turned to gaze apprehensively at the carcass of the building. The groaning sound was soon accompanied by the earth shaking, then two buttresses that had remained standing along the west wall finally fell. They hit the ground, and the stones separated, looking like two huge spinal columns from some improbable dinosaur.

"Was there anyone else inside?" Harald asked.

"I'm not sure. There was so much confusion," said the priest. "I certainly hope not."

He looked around the area, quietly counting heads.

"Well, search the area," Harald told him.

Harald counted out four of his firefighters and sent them toward the rubble. The men still had full face masks on, protecting themselves from all the dirt, soot and gases rising from the stones though the fires in the church had been put out. Gingerly, they poked and prodded their way into the now exposed sanctuary.

The east wall collapsed, smashing pews and timbers. Long rails of ancient oak poked up through the dressed stones, making them look like huge hors d'oeuvres. The other walls had fallen outward, pulling most of the roof off to one side and exposing what was left of the sanctuary to the darkening sky. Standing alone at the back of the church, the altar was still somewhat intact. If anyone had been left inside, they were surely buried underneath the enormous stone blocks that had been cut by hand so long before.

The woman cradling the chalice made her way over to Harald. Wisps of gray hair waved about her lined forehead, peppered with bits of ash.

"I'm really sorry we couldn't save it…your church that is," Harald said to her.

She smoothed her sweater over the chalice, hoisting its weight up a little higher in her arms so she could free her one hand, which she used to sweep the tousled hair from her brow.

"Maybe it was not such a bad thing," she said, "God does things for a reason."

Harald was surprised by her statement but noticed some of the other parishioners nodding in agreement. They crossed themselves with her as they watched the firefighters poking through the rubble. More than one person throughout the centuries had thought the old cathedral to be haunted, much like many old buildings in Europe.

Stories were told of a pitiful wailing heard coming from deep within the cathedral. Several investigations had been launched to determine what this banshee might be, but nothing was ever found, or so the investigators claimed. A few witnesses swore that this apparently unhappy spirit had tried to speak to them, screaming as if buried deep in the earth, but they could never make out anything intelligible because the words were so muffled.

Legend said a criminal of some note was supposedly buried under the church, and it was he who cried out from time to time, furious that an entire church was sitting on top of him. Nothing was ever confirmed, and the rumors persisted for centuries, growing more frightening with each passing year.

Harald looked towards the western horizon, shielding his eyes as he strained to see through the smoke and few remaining walls of flame inside the factory. The sun had slid out of sight, setting that edge of the world ablaze with a deep red light.

"It's going to get dark soon," Harald spoke into his mic. "See if you can hurry this up."

Aaron, one of the firefighters, turned and waved back to Harald, then hurried his men along to search for anyone in the church. The men moved slowly, methodically, scouring the area, looking for potential survivors and making sure they kept eyes on each other. So far, they had not found anyone, dead or alive.

Curiously, towards the back of the church, a small portion of the wall remained with a section of stained glass window still set securely in it. Aaron had seen similar bizarre images in photos from when entire buildings were demolished, but a chair or the stairwell would remain intact. One photo he had seen, which made him laugh as a child, showed a house, completely destroyed except for the plumbing to the second floor, topped by a sink with a shaving kit still sitting on its edge.

He studied the fragment of window and noticed it showed part of the story of St. Norbert, thrown from his horse as a thunderbolt hit the ground in front of them. According to the story of St. Norbert, he had been unimpressed by God and the church, but after his near brush with death, where he lay unconscious for over an hour, he was humbled and left his life of excess behind to become a priest.

For Aaron, familiar with the German saint because of Sunday school, this particular bit of imagery was quite powerful. Based on the uneven textures of the glass and the heavy leading, he figured the window had to have been at least two, maybe three, hundred years old. Whoever the artist had been, he demonstrated a tremendous amount of skill. The bolt of lightning, coming from the fist of God partially hidden in a cloud, looked deadly. The few rays of remaining light, already red from the setting sun and remaining bits of fire, hit the window at just the right angle, and that bolt of lightning glowed. He could see its exact shape cast on the smashed stone blocks below.

The fist of God surely blew this place apart, Aaron thought to himself.

The other men—Willem, Daniel and Friedrich—thoroughly searched the church. They had done this procedure many times before and knew the drill inside and out. They kept abreast of one another, always in at least one other person's line of vision. In a building as damaged as this one, anything could happen. The last thing any rescuer wanted to have happen was to need a rescue themselves.

Every few minutes the group paused while Willem called out.

"Hello! Is anybody there?"

They would all stand absolutely still, listening for even the smallest sound that might indicate a survivor lost in all of that rubble. So far, they heard nothing except the sounds of the massively heavy timbers shifting on top of each other.

A slight breeze blew over damaged items in the church and, if the wind passed by just so, produced an eerie whistling sound. That sound was unsettling to Daniel, and he imagined specters from all the dead bodies previously displayed there during sad funerals drifting along behind them, emitting the freakish noise. He knew that in quite a few old cathedrals like this one, some of the first priests were actually buried in the floor so that their pious nature, even in death, would add to the sanctity of the place. All it did was creep him out even further, and he seriously hoped that they did not stumble across one of them, pried from its ancient burial spot.

Daniel drifted farther to the right. He had come across several huge timbers that had been part of the ceiling, the ancient wood black from centuries of candles burning in the church. He crouched down and peered in through the interlaced timbers, shining his flashlight about, but only picked up more fragments of broken glass and a few pieces of smashed statuary. The grim, marble face of St. Bartholoma stared back at him, but he could not see any people in there.

The other firefighters waited for him while he looked. Once he straightened up, he waved them on, and they continued their sweep of the church.

Daniel had to walk completely around the huge pile of wood to get back in line with the other three men. He stepped up and over a shattered pew, then fell into a deep stairwell, the stone steps worn from centuries of use. As he tumbled down them, he cried out to the other men who quickly came to his rescue.

Daniel rolled to the bottom. The deepening gloom of twilight prevented much light from getting down here. Thankful he had cradled it to his chest so it would not shatter, he shone his flashlight about, looking for anyone or anything. The room he had landed in had a low ceiling, typical of most medieval structures, and little decoration, unlike the sanctuary above.

The other three men reached him.

"You okay?" Aaron cried out through his mask.

Daniel nodded that he was and rose to his feet, casting his light about again. The others joined him.

Toward the back of the chamber, many of the stones had been cracked by the blast. Daniel wandered over to the fissures and noticed that an entire section had fallen away, revealing a hidden passageway leading further into the basement of the church. He ran his gloved hands over the edges of the rock, feeling the sharpness where they had split in half. He peered down into the passageway and noticed the dust covering everything. Clearly the area had been blocked to prevent anyone from getting in.

"I wonder why it was sealed off like this," David said.

"Who knows," said Willem. "Maybe it leaked or something."

They gave the unusual passageway a final look and turned to go.

Then they heard the sound.

The hair on the back of each man's neck immediately stood up. Heat from the blasted stones and the small fires still burning next door had warmed the area, but they each felt a chill that tightened their bellies and pulled their testicles up closer to their bodies.

"Did you hear that?" Daniel asked.

Willem nodded while Aaron spun about, shining his light everywhere. Friedrich stood stock still, listening intently.

"Someone must have fallen down here somehow," Daniel cried out.

"No, no, it's just the timbers, settling on each other," Friedrich disagreed.

There were no further sounds.

"Is anyone down here?" Aaron briefly lifted his facemask so that his shout could be heard further down the hallway.

No one replied.

"Come on, let's get out of here. This place gives me the creeps," shouted Friedrich.

The men turned to leave, picking their way over broken stones back to the old stairwell. The wailing sound hit them again, and they froze, trying hard to pinpoint its location.

"Someone is down there," Aaron stated calmly as he headed for the weird passageway.

"How?" asked Willem. "That hallway hasn't seen the light of day for what, century's maybe. Who could be down there?"

"Well," replied Friedrich, "the floor was really torn apart up there. Someone may have fallen through."

Daniel thought about this for a moment, then agreed that it was certainly a possibility. He just did not like being in this basement. Something about the place gave him a bad chill. He had searched through burned rubble dozens of times since he became a firefighter some twenty years earlier and had found numerous people, most burned beyond recognition. They startled him at first until his professional demeanor took hold, but not this time. Something seemed wrong.

At first, he did not move and gave serious thought to turning and bolting back up the stairs, but he could not abandon the others. He would be labeled a coward for the rest of his life, and they would be right for labeling him such.

The four of them headed for the passageway, moving cautiously down the long, narrow space. At the end, they stepped out into another chamber similar to the one they had just come through, but even more dusty and unused. The stones were not worn looking like they were elsewhere in the church; they looked like they had just been cut days before instead of decades.

Off to one side was a large horse-drawn coach, hundreds of years old. How or why it was down in the small space was a mystery. There were other relics in the room: life-sized stone statues of saints, rotting banners, damaged pews and other assorted junk. At the far end stood an elaborate-looking door which had been covered over in stone. The blast had weakened the mortar near the base, and the entire affair had toppled over, almost intact.

There was no one in the room, so they moved towards the door. Aaron studied it as closely as he had studied the stained glass fragment of St. Norbert above. It was very old, with enormous metal fixtures holding the wood together, so very typical of medieval architecture. A huge, rusted padlock and hand wrought chains were wound tightly around the handles. With one blow of an axe, Willem sliced neatly through the old metal, which fell to the ground, rusty powder billowing out after the impact.

Daniel pushed gently against the doors. They were at least eight feet tall and together more than twice as wide. They gave slightly but had lain against each other for so many years that it was clear they would not yield so easily. The hinges had stretched slightly, so the doors themselves helped hold each other up like praying hands pressed tightly together at the palms.

Again, Aaron cried out.

"Is there anyone in here?!"

The four of them stood silently, heads bowed, waiting for the slightest whisper.

"Yes, I am here," a croaking voice called out, distinctly but quietly, from deep inside the vault.

That was all they needed. Galvanized, the men threw their weight against the old doors. They swung open with difficulty, revealing a large room with a vaulted ceiling. Daniel guessed they were under the altar area of the church, where the floor above was the heaviest, so it needed vaulting like this down here to support it.

They stepped into the room, casting their lights about.

"Where are you?!" Aaron called out.

No one answered.

All four men were thankful they had masks and oxygen with them. The room was starved for it. Dust lay inches thick over everything. Oddly, there were no signs of rodents or even insects, not even a spider web. Just an eerie layer of dust built up over everything.

They stepped further into the room, and then saw the gap in the ceiling towards the back. The main stones of the altar had indeed shifted, and a large crack allowed a bit of light below. Aaron looked up and saw the St. Norbert window above. The light through the colored glass made interesting patterns on the dusty floor.

"I don't see anyone in here!" Willem called out, frustrated.

"If there was, we would know where they are. Look how deep this dust is. It would be like leaving tracks in the snow," said Friedrich.

Confused, they stood in the center of the room.

"Look at that." Daniel pointed at the floor.

A trail was worn into the stone, as if someone had paced back and forth, wearing it down. Dust had settled there as well, but not as thick as in other areas of the room.

In a corner at the far end, under the rib of an enormous vault, a strange shape rested, covered in grime. Their flashlights passed quickly over it, and the men assumed it was just a statue. It looked very much like it could have been a stone gargoyle the way it sat hunched over, head slid down behind arms wrapped tightly around the knees.

As the men looked away, moving further into the room to look for the survivor, the gargoyle's head rose, and its eyes snapped open. Dust, like fine snow, flew from its lashes. Its skin rustled and crackled, like old parchment, but its eyes felt wide and alive."

Slowly the figure rose, carefully watching the firefighters moving toward the other end of the room on their mission of mercy. The figure looked like a man—gaunt, pale, but a man nonetheless. At least, at one time he had been a man.

Nearly seven hundred years ago, he had lived as a man in this beautiful region of Germany. His name was Villicus Shanks, and he had been a merchant who specialized in importing rare and priceless goods from the Far East. His business was successful, his life full of social events and women, so many women. His outgoing personality and business savvy, however, attracted the attention of others, a species that moves only at night, in the dark, preying on the living.

He had fallen into their fold and loved the attention they lavished on him, unaware of their intentions. Villicus marveled at their slow, easy way of laughing, the enormous amount of money they spent, the confidence and grace they exuded. He emulated all that they did and wished he could be like them, something he often confided to the oldest of the group.

It is hard not to envy the vampire. They move with the elegance of an acrobat, as if their joints were oiled with mercury or silicon. Their eyes, colored brightly, dart about, as though they can see more than what is there. In close proximity to one, a human desires only to lie in its arms and let come what may.

The quarter-full moon that peered through the cracks the evening of the cathedral fire was the same face in the sky from so many years ago when Villicus met his new friends on the banks of a nearby lake. The water, so still, reflected the moon, the stars and nearby mountains.

They had lit a grand bonfire and gathered around it. A girl was produced, a lovely young thing who had been lured away from her home in a nearby village. She was given to Villicus to take pleasure in first. He took her slowly, enjoying her to the fullest, finally shuddering to a climax deep inside her body.

Villicus looked up at that moment to see the face of one of his new friends hovering close to his. The young girl underneath him stirred strangely, then reached hungrily for this being who grasped her hair, wrenched her head back and ripped out her throat while Villicus was still inside her.

Horrified, Villicus backed away, but he was grasped from behind and held, forced to watch the girl die. When the deed was done, his new friends sat in a semi-circle around him, watching him closely. Their eyes darkened to black pools, blood dripping from their now exposed fangs.

They did not move, did not breathe or even shift their eyes. Villicus did not know which was more terrifying, how preternaturally still they were or how blood still drooled from their teeth and fell to the ground, sending up tiny crowns of dust.

He understood, although not a word was spoken. They were showing him what they were, and so they sat there, stock still, watching him carefully. He knew he had the opportunity to walk away if that was his will. That was their gift to him, letting him decide what his fate would be.

He remained.

And so they made him as they were. One grasped his wrist and slowly bit into the artery. The other one, the oldest one, shoved his own wrist into Villicus's mouth. Instinctively, he bit down with his rounded teeth and roughly parted the flesh. They smiled when they saw his reaction. Blood filled his mouth, and he drank voraciously as if he had never suffered from thirst before this night, the blood pouring down Villicus's throat all that would quench it.

During the transition from human to vampire, he could feel his teeth lengthen and sharpen. With renewed strength, even as his birth life slipped away, he tore deeper into the flesh of this ancient creature crouched before him whose origin was described in the book of Genesis. This being standing before Villicus was a Nephilim, a damned creature born of a human woman but sired by an angel.

Finally, the creature rose and slowly but forcefully pulled his wrist from Villicus's mouth. Even as he pulled his arm back, Villicus was startled to see the brutal wound he had created drawing itself closed and appearing to heal.

And then the creature was gone.

Disappointed, Villicus looked about, wanting to see him again, wanting so badly to touch him and savor the blood that tasted like the origins of life itself. His disappointment gave way to a yearning that threatened to consume him with unquenchable fire.

He rose to his feet and felt gargantuan but light as a feather at the same time. It took him a couple of steps to get his balance. Slowly, Villicus turned in a circle and finally saw his maker, the dark being that had so changed him forever, perched far up in a pine tree, standing on the very end of a branch that would not even support the weight of the tiniest of songbirds.

He was…his name was…*No! Don't think it!*

Villicus had trained himself again and again never to say or think his maker's name, the vile creature who brought him into this existence and then sought to end him. Villicus fought to maintain himself and take care of the tasks at hand. It was dawning on him that his misery may indeed be coming to an end, so he needed to pay attention.

There would certainly be plenty of time for him to think about the last seven hundred years and how he had been forced into his predicament. It was hard though, so very hard, for him to remain calm and stay so focused like this when all he wanted to do was howl and tear through the men, destroy anything and everything he got his hands on.

As the rest of those dark beings had watched him that first night, their eyes dark and their bodies frozen unnaturally, so Villicus watched the firefighters. The eyes are the windows to a man's soul, but a vampire has no soul, nor is he a man, so this dark countenance, amber hues turning to inky black, was fitting.

Villicus shook his body once, rapidly, to eject the filth clinging to him. He opened his mouth and pumped his jaw a few times like a fish might scour the surface of a pond. His teeth, unused for so long, lengthened in the front. He clacked them together, quietly, then ran his tongue lovingly over the points. Piercing the end of his own tongue, he allowed a bit of his vampire blood to spill into his mouth. The sensation thrilled him. He nearly groaned with anticipation of what was to come but kept his silence.

He had waited so long, so very long, hoping another human would cross his path, and there were four of them. Perfect prey. He could wait another minute.

Although gaunt, starving and looking like a half-stuffed rag doll with badly tanned leather for skin, Villicus still moved with the speed and grace of a young cheetah. Quickly, but silently, he glided across the room to Daniel, who was closest. Gently, Villicus wrapped his arms around the man's chest and then slid his facemask off, letting it fall to the ground. Oxygen streamed from the mask, carving patterns into the downy dust layered on the stone floor.

Daniel seemed startled at first, but rapidly succumbed to Villicus's exuded charm, his inherent vampire way of seducing the prey into willingness. Together, the two men backed into a corner. Villicus looked quickly to make sure the others were unaware of the events unfolding, then squeezed his eyes shut as he squeezed the man tightly in his arms. He could feel the pounding heart through the tightly bound flesh and pulled his arms closer still. Ribs snapped and his prey's breath moved in and out of the body in wet, ragged bursts, struggling to get air to sustain a life that would soon be extinguished.

Daniel's eyes bugged from their sockets, and blood dripped from his nose, down across his lips which were beginning to froth. His distressed, huffing breaths blew the blood into the air, creating a fine spray. Villicus let go with one hand and extended his fingers, letting the bloody mist coat them. He marveled at the site of the gore, slicking his stark, bony claws, and could wait no longer.

Villicus ripped into his neck, tearing the side of Daniel's throat out. Opening his jaws as wide as they would go, he could feel his ancient, worn skin tearing from the effort and felt the hot blood pouring down his parched throat. Fire rushed into his limbs, and the wounds in his face healed instantly from the infusion.

Renewed with blood and amazed he had survived so many centuries trapped deep in the earth, he turned to the other three men and, one by one, took their lives.

They went quietly, more or less. Aaron and Willem were the last to die. Stunned to silence, they could not believe the horror they had unearthed. Friedrich died in front of them, a bizarre look of ecstasy on his face which quickly faded like the end of day after the sun sets.

Willem, in shock, walked willingly into Villicus's deadly embrace. Aaron died on his knees, looking up at the St. Norbert window. Villicus allowed him to cross himself before he ripped the arteries in his neck open.

On the surface, Harald called repeatedly into his mic for the men who had disappeared inside the ruins of the church. Down below, Villicus, now satiated and feeling power and strength returning to his severely starved vampire body, listened with head cocked at the voice coming from inside Aaron's clothing.

He poked and prodded until he found Aaron's mic and held it, marveling at the way it vibrated in his hand whenever Harald's voice issued from it.

He picked up one of their facemasks, feeling the drift of oxygen still pumping from the reservoir. Other things, tiny details, caught his eye: how their clothes were made, the fillings in their teeth, the precise detail in their simple jewelry, and even the slight traces of aftershave one of them wore.

Twilight had succumbed to night, and gathering clouds were obscuring the stars. Rain was approaching with leaden clouds that promised lightning and roaring thunder.

Villicus, completely ready to leave his living tomb, took Daniel's firefighters coat and put it on. It felt good to have new clothing on his back. His own was mostly rotted away. From Aaron, he took his boots.

Through the crack in the ceiling, Villicus could see faint flashes of lightning snake through the sky, illuminating the stained glass window. Before he climbed to the surface, Villicus, with his renewed strength, buried Aaron and the others beneath the stone floor. He could not risk leaving any clue he had been there. That had been the way of existence for the vampire since first they were formed.

The firefighters' bodies would never be found. He had laughed while he buried them. *At least,* he thought to himself, *they were interred in consecrated ground.*

Villicus looked around one last time at the room and shook his head, trying to forget the sound of so many hymns repeating, over and over again. What dreadful voices these Christians had!

Running, something he had not done for some time, he raced toward one of the stone ribs, climbing effortlessly up into the vault and then out through the fissure. From his new vantage point above ground, he crouched and took in the lay of the land.

Gone was the church, lying in a rubble around him. *Good... GOOD!* He was so thrilled that he had not only been released from his prison, but it had been destroyed in the process.

The reek of the factory next door assaulted his senses, but he quickly ignored it, seeing it was not a threat. He saw the people gathered nearby and noticed another search party approaching the ruin. Then he saw Stuttgart below and froze. So many lights burning in the night, and what were those!

Motorized vehicles glided through the streets. What mad sorcery had spawned those diabolical entities? Villicus could smell a horrible stench wafting up from the city, presumably from those odd beasts.

Looking over the city more, he took in the massive buildings and factories. Neon lights sparkled with bursts of clear, multiple colors. Was he looking at more fire or some sort of gypsy magic trick?

With startled fascination, he quickly turned to spy a news helicopter circling the area near the church and incinerated factory, still sending up thick, roiling black columns of reeking smoke. The flying machine came low not far from him, sending a Nightsun light over the landscape of shattered beams, old fashioned materials and medieval furniture scrambled together with the shattered ugly remnants of metal and plastic from the more modern factory.

He ducked out of sight from that probing, intense light, brighter than what he remembered the sun to be. Whatever it was, he instinctively feared it. He cowered, absolutely still along the base of a destroyed wall, watching it dart back and forth, until the helicopter moved out of the area.

What manner of machines had man created while he had been entombed? His mind racing, he had to hurry. He had to get back down among them. What secrets and surprises did they have in store for him to discover, then take and use as he pleased?

The years of waiting were over. Those who had imprisoned him, the same who had made him, must be found and dealt with. Villicus had a purpose again. He had survived. His vampire body and senses intact, he turned quietly, without fanfare, and disappeared over the hill into the dark.

Chapter Two

The fires on the hill still glowed cherry red with a fierce, golden white heart. More helicopters, carrying news crews, raced back and forth between the city and the site of the blaze.

Villicus pushed on through the night, stopping from time to time to marvel at the winged creations spinning madly above. To him, they appeared as ferocious demons, dipping and hovering, screaming with their jet engine noise and puking nauseating exhaust into the air. He picked up a small rock and hurled it with inhuman strength at one of them. It clipped a rotor blade, sending the airship hurtling sideways.

The helicopter, too damaged to attempt a safe landing, slammed sideways into a large field of carefully cultivated asparagus. It pounded itself partway into the ground as the rotors released all of their energy and finally slowed to a stop. A few people pulled themselves from the wreckage and ran or crawled away before it burst into flame. Villicus found this incredibly funny.

"Why do these modern people make everything to burn?"

A couple of other news copters zipped over the wreckage, igniting their own Nightsun lights. Villicus watched the wreckage burn for another moment, enjoying the fact that as fascinating and magical as it seemed, he killed it with just a rock. His spirits lifted more, realizing that he was probably going to be able to survive, and survive well, out in this noisy explosive realm.

Avoiding the Nightsun lights, he turned again and started a slow, easy lope towards Stuttgart.

Since the death of the firefighters, Villicus was still morphing into his full vampire state. His hair, once a matted, filthy nightmare, now shone a glistening black and swung freely between his shoulder blades. He pulled the elaborate silver ring that held his hair back and shook his mane loose, then deftly reformed his ponytail again, high on the back of his head.

When he had still been a living man, Villicus had seen the hairstyle on men in an Asian painting a merchant had brought back from the Far East. The image showed warriors, with grimacing white faces, jet-black hair and slanted, red-rimmed eyes hunting down and killing a massive boar. Villicus loved the ferocity of it.

He had shown the painting to a local jeweler who created the hair tie for him from twisted silver and copper, fashioned into a taught U-shaped bow pulled together at the top with fine, thin silver chains dangling elegantly about three inches from the crown of the tail. When he shook his head, he loved to hear the tinkle of the silver chains. To him, it sounded like coins kissing each other in a fine silk purse, a sound he never tired of.

Villicus delighted in wearing his hair like this, especially when he attended parties. He loved to greet women, as they sat perched like elegant, little china dolls on the edge of damask covered settees, by leaning over and delicately brushing his lips across the backs of their perfect, tiny hands. His hair would fall forward, sweeping over their fingertips, captured sweetly in his own massive hand. He would look up into their faces and see a faint blush steal across their porcelain cheeks, their mouths parting delicately, at the seductive sensation of his hair brushing across their pampered skin.

Later, one of these lovely ladies would be his partner for the night. Villicus had been an aggressive lover, sometimes leaving his partner with bites and bruises if she responded with equal passion. Always, he would leave her before the sun came up on a new day.

The women drifted in and out of his life, and not one of them ever became a permanent fixture. He was not ready for love, his friends often said, only lust, and they joked about his prowess, his hunger for women. Sometimes he thought about that, wondering if he was a slave to sex. Decided he was, so he would dine voraciously until he had his fill.

He loved sex, but when he assumed his existence as one of the undead, he had to leave all of that behind. The memories of those couplings often haunted him, infuriated him, because he could no longer taste the joys of the flesh as he drained the body of its life. He often hunted women to try to regain that sense of sexual conquest he had relished as a man, but as a vampire, he could do little more than kill them. In agony, he would stroke the flesh of his willing victim, trying to rekindle that sense of lust, but the only sensation he had was of being a driven beast, pushed to kill, to steal life.

Infuriated, he would beg her to help him find that feeling again, to be able to love her body and turn her skin to fire. But as he stared into the vacant, hollow eyes of his victim, realizing again and again he could never have that passion back, he would rip her throat out, gulping down pints of blood, never taking his eyes from hers as he watched the light go out. Oftentimes his victim died, shuddering in his arms, from the rapid blood loss and the massive orgasm he could give her with his fingers as she passed over the threshold. At least he could still give them that!

As a vampire he could not enjoy carnal pleasures, neither could he feel remorse. When he had been a man, he enjoyed the closeness of her after he had orgasmed deep inside her body and always kept some part of his skin in touch with hers. But as a vampire, once his rage was spent, he would rapidly dispose of the corpse, ripping it to pieces, feeding it to pigs or wolves and walking away without even remembering her name, if he even knew it in the first place.

Was he no longer a man?

Certainly, there were men who treated women like objects, but Villicus had not when he was still alive. Every time he loved a woman, he did so with all his senses and still marveled at her when they were done with their passion, but as a vampire, she became little more than an object for him to vent his rage on and a source for his unquenchable thirst for blood. From understanding that difference in his nature, he knew he was no longer a man.

He still had his love for money and for power. Vampire life had not altered that, except he had become better at acquiring it. The vampires he had known in the day used to joke about that. Lose one sense and the others sharpen. For the made ones, their longing for the taste of food, wine or the painful, sweet sensations of sex was replaced with violent rages when they took their victims.

Often, when they were done feeding, it was hard to recognize their victim had been human at all. It took centuries for the vampire to become inured to his or her fate and embrace what the existence offered. Their so-called lives in those early years were a raging storm of highs, their incredible strength and increased ability to see, hear and smell juxtaposed with the painful loss of carnal pleasures and the ability to truly care for anyone or anything.

Of course, there were the Nephelim. They were the original ones, bastard children borne at the dawn of man from the unholy coupling of angels and mortal women. Legend had it that Goliath was a Nephilim. Certainly Bale was.

Bale.

Bale!

Villicus had not dared to even think that name for centuries and fought so hard while he was escaping the church to keep it from poisoning his thoughts. He had driven that name from his memories, choosing instead to play over and over again in his mind a storm he had witnessed from atop a belfry in the northern part of Italy.

As easily as a thought, he had scaled the side of the church when he knew the storm was approaching. He hovered up there, gripping the narrow edge of the bell tower as a powerful wind whipped down through the Italian Alps, seeking the sea. The first bolts of lightning ripped through the sky, highlighting the purple-white clouds. It was night, of course, and a full golden moon, straining to be seen through the wind torn clouds, added to the amazing sight of the surreal light show.

That display of nature had sustained Villicus as he finally crouched down in the corner of his prison beneath the cathedral, after having spent the first two hundred years pacing and wearing a pathway in the stone floor. He slid down, taking nearly a full week to do so, and let the movie in his head play over and over again, waiting for death to arrive or madness to overtake him.

Neither did.

And now, he stood in an open field, letting the wind move his hair about, tasting life on his pierced tongue from every angle he turned. So many humans he could sense! So much food, so much sport!

Bale!

The name ripped through his skull again, driving him momentarily to his knees.

Bale, the one who had made him. A Nephilim. An original one. Not a giant as Goliath had been, but Nephilim none-the-less. An evil one. A killer of souls without a soul himself.

Bale had been his mentor as well as his maker. Slick, sensuous, a being that moved like heavy silk fluttering on a warm breeze, he stalked the streets and alleys of each city in Europe he chose to conquer, taking what he wanted, forcing men and vampires alike to grovel at his feet.

And then there was Nikonar, the beautiful, golden, graceful one from the north, a friend who had been made just a scant one hundred years before Villicus had been, also by Bale. It was Nikonar who had lured Villicus to St. Bartholoma's, then still a small stone church with a rude altar of hand-hewn stone adorned with huge, tallow candles that reeked of the animal fat from which they had been rendered.

He and Nikonar often spoke of the war that had been raging, a war that most humans were oblivious to. Nor would they care, as miserable as most of their lives were, because at that time in Europe, there were more wolves than humans. That hideous plague which had ridden in on the rats' fleas was killing off the people by the thousands. The vampires' food was being depleted, and wars between them raged nightly as they fought over the few healthy, remaining herds. Villicus assumed Nikonar wanted to again talk about ways to end the war, and he was amused at the location chosen for that night.

Nikonar sat off to one side, waiting for Villicus, who strode into the narthex those hundreds of years ago.

"Why here?" Villicus had asked.

"I like the quiet," Nikonar responded, watching him impassively from a pew where he was sprawled comfortably over the worn wood.

"Since when do you like solitude?"

Nikonar rose to his feet, smoothing out his luxurious coat. He stamped his feet lightly on the age polished stone floor, pushing his feet deeply into the expensive boots.

"Since the humans wail so much," Nikonar explained.

"Mothers and children are dying."

"I know. The stench is unbelievable. Everyone's dying. And since when did you care about mothers and their bastard children?"

Villicus played with one of the fat candles burning by the altar. He poked his finger into the flame, letting his flesh blacken, then pulled it out and watched as his skin resumed its perfect, pearly hue.

"I don't," Villicus went on, sounding bored. "Nikonar, what do you want?"

The Russian vampire laughed loudly, startling the pigeons roosting high in the eaves. They fluttered about, then settled down in the rafters again after shedding a fine, downy snow of feathers that floated through the heavy church air.

He toyed with one small feather, balancing it on a fingertip, then let it drift away. He motioned for Villicus to follow him.

The church was made from heavy, hand-hewn black stones nearly one hundred years away from being turned into the massive St. Bartholoma's Cathedral. Instead of the magnificent stained glass windows that would be shattered by an exploding fertilizer factory, narrow slit windows allowed fine beams of moonlight to paint patterns on the stone floor.

Nikonar moved to the wall behind the altar where a few large tapestries, the only source of warmth in the building, hung flush with the wall. He pulled one forward, revealing a narrow open doorway leading into the black depths below the church. Before passing through the opening, he noticed the tiny flame burning next to the small wooden box holding the Host.

He quickly snatched the flame away, leaving the area dark.

"Where are we going?" Villicus asked.

"Oh, my boy," Nikonar sounded pained. "You ask too many questions. Down here, we may have a solution to our problem."

"We?"

"The royal we," Nikonar quickly interjected.

Both vampires laughed loudly at the joke, for indeed, they felt themselves to be royalty in the world.

Nikonar moved ahead of Villicus, stepping down with confidence onto the narrow, slick steps of a curved staircase. Even in the total dark, their eyes adjusted to the absence of light. Villicus spotted movement off to one side and could make out a small gathering of rats, nesting in some rags in the corner. Fearfully they studied the two vampires, then scurried off to the far corners of the basement, not wanting to be near these unholy creatures.

"The war must end, Villicus."

"And how shall it end? Have you found a cure for the plague?"

Villicus pointed to the rats running off in all directions.

"No. I think not. Time will cure that, as with all things."

They moved through a narrow passageway, past piles of crates and old furniture into the doorway of another chamber where Nikonar stopped. He pointed deep inside.

"We found it in there."

"Again, this *we*. I must tell you though, I am intrigued. Just what is it you think *we* have found down here?"

Villicus moved past Nikonar, deeper into the chamber. Standing in the middle of the room was a stone statue of St. Sebastian, his pain-wracked and bound body pierced over and over again with arrows chronicling the death of the martyr. Villicus ran his fingers along the edge of one of the shafts, then looked back at Nikonar who stood almost more still than the statue, his blonde hair curling elegantly over his velvet clad shoulders.

Using just his fingertip, Villicus poked the large, heavy statue causing it to rock precariously on its base.

"And what is all this now?"

"We thought he would be suitable company for you," Nikonar said.

In the dark, as if a dark upon a dark, Villicus saw a shadow move up behind Nikonar. The shadow became more solid, and he recognized the visage of his maker, Bale. He stood nearly as tall as Nikonar, with a dark countenance, delicate skin, a strong jaw, but then there was something, something different about his appearance. He looked human enough, but it was almost as if he wore the mask of a man, hiding his true Nephilim appearance behind a thin tissue of human flesh and closely cropped dark hair. His eyes, blazing blue, stared at Villicus.

Villicus stared into those eyes, as always, feeling a sense of revulsion mingled with blind love. What did his maker have in store for him?

Nikonar backed away, looking down, avoiding Villicus's puzzled expression.

Bale slowly pulled the heavy wooden doors closed, all the while smiling sweetly at Villicus. Sensing danger, Villicus flew forward with vampire strength and speed, but Bale moved faster, slamming the doors shut.

"Bale! What is this!? What have I done?"

There was no response from the other side of the door, just the sounds of heavy stones being moved up against the door and a wet, slopping noise.

Villicus clawed at the doors, gouging out chunks of wood much like someone buried alive might rip into the lid of their own coffin. Surely, this was meant to be his tomb, and he wanted no part of it.

He grasped the doors in his fingertips, pulling them forward, trying to break Bale's grasp on the other side. The doors parted slightly, and Villicus could see Nikonar working rapidly, slapping mortar onto dressed stones as he built a wall across the entrance.

For a brief moment he and Bale made eye contact, and in that moment, Villicus saw and knew the truth, that Bale feared him. Momentarily stunned by this revelation, Villicus lost his grip on the door. Bale seized this opportunity by shoving the doors hard, throwing Villicus backward across the room into the statue of St. Sebastian. The arrows that pierced the stone body of the saint also pierced Villicus's back, holding him fast against the cold, hard body. Villicus howled, causing the rafters in the room to quake, and dust rained down on all of them.

The pain for him was startling, fierce, and caused bright flashes to sear his eyes. He shook his head and howled in pain again, struggling to pull himself off of the stone arrowheads that impaled him. Bale stood in the door, watching him, his face an unreadable mask. Nikonar paused for a moment to watch Villicus's demise, but Bale turned on him, hissing his disapproval. Nikonar quickly resumed his work. The wall was halfway up the door.

Bale pulled the doors closed again, and Villicus could hear the sound of metal chains being wound through the handles and a padlock being locked into place. The stones were being slammed harder and faster against the door. He could see the wood shake from the massive weight being built up against them.

Stretching his feet, he found purchase on the stone floor, now slick with his blood. Villicus, screaming from the pain and howling obscenities at Bale and Nikonar, managed to push himself upward enough to take pressure off the arrows sticking into his back. He fell forward and hit the ground hard.

Crawling forward on hands and knees, he reached the door and pounded on it.

"Bale!"

The sounds of the stones sliding into place came from up near the top. They were almost done.

"No! Don't leave me here!"

Then silence.

"Nikonar? For the love of...me?"

Silence.

Villicus ran his fingers along the bottom of the door, and although he could grasp the wood and pull slightly, he was unable to open the huge doors. The door opening inward but being fastened from the outside and covered over by tons of stone had sealed him inside.

By then, he could feel the wounds in his back beginning to close over, but the pain was still excruciating. He crawled back to the base of the statue of St. Sebastian and, realizing he was entombed now, bent over and licked up his own blood from the stone floor. Grit pasted against his tongue along with the blood already cold and clotting. He spat the first mouthful out but forced himself to continue to lick it back up. He could ill afford to go without his only sustenance.

The statue did not last very long. Villicus had beaten it to dust within the first year of his imprisonment, imagining he was slaughtering Bale or Nikonar. Any spiders or rats unfortunate enough to have been entombed with him provided him with some blood, but there were very few of them, and before long he was going through the gut-ripping hunger pangs only a vampire can know.

He wanted to die. Over and over again, he lay on the ground, pleading to God to take him, to let him die. His body convulsed, bending and twisting into excruciating shapes as the pangs tore into him. He cried and howled, but no one came close. Through the thick stone walls, his cries were muffled and sounded like the distant rumblings of thunder or possibly a demon haunting the depths of the old structure. As the years slipped by and the church grew and grew into the massive cathedral that finally perched above his head, the very act of enlarging the building put more and more distance between himself and any would be rescuer.

Oh, to be sure, over the next several years, Villicus tested the bonds of his prison again and again until his body shriveled to the point where he could barely move. How he survived was a mystery to him. The centuries had turned him into a gaunt, nearly lifeless scarecrow, but as soon as the firefighters neared him, his vision cleared, and he knew his purpose was to rip their throats out and drink his fill. When he cut into the first artery and felt the hot blood spurt into his mouth, Villicus had nearly fainted from the sheer pleasure of it. Nothing ever had tasted so sweet, so satisfying to him. He wrapped his lips around the open wound and sucked so intensely his tongue slid deep into the artery and he could feel the cut edge flapping against his teeth. He had ripped into the flesh, burying his face in the gore, loving every second of it.

A distant rumbling startled Villicus out of his reverie, and he spun around in the open field again, looking for walls confining him, but realized he was free of the tomb. The fires on the hill were going to burn wickedly all night, and they served as a landmark for him. As long as they were at his back, he was sure he was moving in the right direction. He watched as another spine of stone crumbled on the hill, causing the rumbling sound.

He ran forward across the field again, titling his head back and letting his mouth hang open, enjoying the fresh air blowing across his skin and the wet tissues of his mouth. He could taste the world on his tongue, and it had been too long since he had allowed the world to feed him.

Up ahead, he could see the lights from Stuttgart, not the usual dim, yellowish hue he was used to seeing from tallow candles burning in windows, but brilliant whites and greens, blues and reds, blinking and blinding him with their brightness. He reached the outskirts of the city, keeping to the shadows as he saw cars and buses lumbering around on the hard streets. The sounds of the engines deafened him after so many centuries in solitude. He could hear what he thought was music pounding through the night from a building covered in bright, neon signs.

Such sights, he could barely take it all in. The only thing that had not changed were the people. Whatever fantastic inventions were swirling about him, the people seemed the same. He could control people. He could kill people. They were still his cattle, no matter how overwhelming their inventions seemed to him. Unable to be killed, he moved without fear, knowing that anyone who might confront him would quickly realize his power.

Villicus walked the streets, changed so drastically since he had last wandered them. WWII had destroyed much of the old city, and it had been built back up since then in a modern style, but in some places, parts of the old hung in there. He gravitated toward the older buildings. Some of them he thought he recognized, sandwiched in between modern monstrosities. He would have to find a home soon, some place to sleep during the daylight hours. His tastes ran to the expensive, the elegant, so he moved towards a part of the city that seemed to cater to that.

Turning a corner, he came to a quaint intersection of

cobblestone streets that looked so much like the Germany he remembered he paused, half expecting to see old friends coming toward him. Instead, he saw a group of people sitting outside a café, soft music filtering from the open doorway. Instead of the harsh lights that had bombarded him as he had trekked through the city, the tables were adorned with candles, and the lights from inside the café itself were dimmed. This, he liked.

Moving closer, he saw that the people were sipping crisp, clear wine from gorgeous thin glasses. Villicus reached the first table and tugged a glass away from one of them so he could look at it more closely. The patrons at first started to complain, but he gazed quietly at them. Just letting them look on him, into his blazing amber eyes, usually shut them up. He had done this countless times before. Humans rarely spoke out against him. The only time one defied him when he stared into his eyes, Villicus nearly fell to the ground laughing, realizing the insolent human was blind. The memory brought a small smile to his lips.

He turned the glass around and around, then upside down, spilling the wine onto the ancient cobblestones. Admiring the thinness of the goblet and simple, elegant styling, he pinged his fingers against the sides of the now empty glass and held it up to his ear, enjoying the crystal humming sound it made. Finished with his study, he reached into the wine bucket next to the table, refilled the glass and handed it back to the person he had snatched it from.

"Danke," he said.

Dumbfounded, the people at the table just stared at him. He moved away from them, chuckling, realizing this was his first encounter with humans in centuries, other than meeting with the firefighters, but he was not counting his ripping them to pieces as any kind of meaningful discourse.

His body, feeling stronger by the minute, added to his overall sense of well-being. He had survived, damnit! If he had been a powerful monster prior to his imprisonment, then by God, having walked away from a living hell into this magnificent world buzzing with commerce, technology and many, many people to feed on made him a veritable god too. He was Himself again.

The memory of seeing that fear in Bale's eyes flashed briefly across his mind. It all made sense to him now. His imprisonment had nothing to do with the wars raging between the vampires. In truth, those had been petty boundary squabbles, and the weaker vampires who had been destroyed in the process deserved to be blasted into oblivion. His race was a powerful one and should only encompass the strongest of the breed. Bale feared him because he, Villicus, was smart and strong and could have become even more powerful than a Nephilim. That had been unheard of. The made ones always kowtowed to the original ones. It was an unwritten law, and the Nephilim were never challenged. Bale recognized the potential in Villicus, though—that strength, the ability to amass great wealth and drive monopolies in the very economies that guaranteed the success of the herds. Villicus had been good at toying with his fellow vampires, toppling their little monarchies as he stole their fortunes and their ignorant flocks.

In anger, several of Villicus's contemporaries had complained to Bale, begging him to rein Villicus in, but instead of challenging him, Bale sought merely to wipe him off the face of the earth. Villicus realized that now and embraced his anger towards Bale with grit and passion. He had purpose again.

Seeing a couple watching him from across the courtyard, Villicus made his way over to them and sat down at their table. Startled at first, they quickly regained their composure and, as most well-to-do people react, sought to speak politely to their interloper.

They spoke to him in English.

"Hello," the man said.

Villicus stared at him, his head cocked to one side. He had heard English before, but it took him some time to recall it. Finally, he answered back.

"Hello."

"Are you a fireman?" the woman asked.

Villicus did not understand her, so he simply shook his head no.

"Oh, we weren't sure," she went on, pointing to his firefighters coat and boots. "Were you at a party then?"

He recognized the word party, smiled and nodded.

"Oh," she went on, with more spirit. "Like a costume party? What fun."

The evening ended badly for this couple. Villicus had listened to them prattle on, as they fell more and more under his spell, blathering away loudly in an attempt to make conversation with him. He shredded their throats in a nearby alley, beneath a small neon sign advertising an old-fashioned bakery that claimed their Lebkuchen cookies were the best around.

After he had slaughtered them and tossed their bodies into a nearby sewer, he went through the items he had taken from them. The money he recognized immediately and carefully examined and counted it. He would sort it later and determine the value of it all.

The other trinkets like the watches, he was able to figure out their purpose, but the cell phone completely confounded him. He kept it anyway, recognizing the advanced technology for what it was and realizing he was going to have to learn what these things were. The credit cards, he had no idea what they were for, but kept them. Looking at the man's driver's license and then hers, he kept seeing the name Los Angeles. It intrigued him, for it spoke of angels.

He had discarded the firefighter's coat, donning the man's casual but cleanly tailored jacket instead and draping the woman's expensive silk scarf around his neck, looping it at the neck in a big bow. Thus adorned, with cash and trinkets in his pockets and further infused with fresh blood, he strode deeper into the old part of the city, seeking suitable lodgings for himself. He knew it would not be long before he found a house to his liking, and he would simply dispose of the owner or owners, the way he planned on taking possession of whatever he wanted.

For he was a vampire, and not just any vampire, but one whom a Nephilim feared and sought to destroy. Villicus would take his time, learning how to navigate in this new world and acquire the wealth and toys he needed to amuse himself and control the human herds around him. Then, he would find Bale and treat him to a fate worse than the one he, Villicus Shanks, had just survived.

Chapter Three

The elevator rode silently and efficiently upward, clicking slightly as each floor was reached. Paul Peter Miller stood silently, his eyes closed, as he listened to the horrendous Muzak version of "The Girl from Ipanema" droning on above his head. He held several high-security pouches loosely against his chest with one hand and a custom beverage carrier holding two metal coffee mugs covered with thick, black plastic caps to prevent spillage in his other. The elevator was paneled with expensive, burled Briarwood and carpeted in a thick pile colored the perfect shade of gunmetal blue. The recessed lighting and gold vein marble gave the small car the air of an expensive opium den.

Paul Peter sensed the express elevator was going to stop. He flexed his knees as it sped to a halt and rode out the change in acceleration with practiced ease. The mirrored doors slid open noiselessly on well-oiled tracks just as he opened his eyes and stepped out into the lobby of the Delancey Financial Group, nestled in its stronghold on the 22nd floor of the Marcus Building in Century City, Los Angeles.

The floor was black marble flecked with just enough silver and mica chips to indicate it was real and worth more than any three-bedroom home in the valley. Paul Peter strolled across the perfectly cut and laid tiles, loving the way the heels of his pricey shoes clicked sweetly on the expensive floor. Shoes were his one major indulgence, and he always wore his best to the office, just to hear that clicking sound first thing in the morning.

He walked through the foyer area capped by a high-vaulted ceiling patterned with tiny, exquisitely fashioned tiles in the shape of a bear and a bull. Jilly, their leggy, blonde receptionist, was already at work, perched elegantly on her ergonomic high chair behind the seemingly endless, bare reception table made of sparkling black granite. Her computer/phone system, suspended next to her in a futuristic-looking armature, was held aloft by thin, high-tensile wires so it looked like it hovered magically in space.

Paul Peter nodded crisply to her as he marched past. She responded with a friendly wave as she slid her phone jack in place. Even though the sun was barely cresting the horizon, calls were already flooding in from clients all over the world. Their business day began with the opening chime on Wall Street.

Several icons flashed on her computer screen as she rushed to answer the first call.

"Good morning, Delancey Financial Group," she said, as smoothly as silk.

Paul Peter paused to stare at her with a silly stone face, trying to make her laugh, but she just smiled as she waved him away, nary a crack in her demeanor. He continued through the foyer to the main hallway linking the primary offices. Off to his left was the legal area of the financial group. Paul Peter always averted his eyes as he went past. Lawyers gave him the willies, so he avoided all of them within the group. He continued into trader's territory, and he could hear several of them on the phone already, chasing the bond markets.

"Yeah, I saw that one. Keep away from it, dude. You'll get dinged if you buy that one!" one trader yelled.

"No, no, let that one go. It's dog snot!" another trader shouted.

That made Paul Peter laugh. The dog snot comment referred to a really bad, junk bond. He hoped that the client asking to buy it had a really good reason to want it. Paul Peter breathed a contented sigh as he walked past the trader's area. He felt at home here in this insane, noisy bastion of the free enterprise system.

Walking down the hallway, he passed the huge fishbowl conference room with its sweeping view of the Hollywood Hills. Way off, down to the right, he could just make out the famous Hollywood Sign perched above Beachwood Canyon. He wondered idly which celebs were up and about yet, what coffee they drank, whom or what they were sleeping with and so on.

He reached an office area where his desk sat fronting double doors with the name "Amanda Brax" on them in bronze letters. He walked to the doors, looked around to make sure no one could see him, and then tapped them lightly with his forehead.

From inside, he heard someone say, "Come on in. It's open."

Paul Peter eased the door open with his foot and entered Amanda's office. She was sitting off to the right at a large computer console showing several monitors tuned to different financial markets from around the world.

"Good morning, Paul," she said brightly.

"Morning, Ms. Brax."

He called her that every morning, and every morning it made her smile.

He plopped the courier bundles down on her desk, one of which hit with a substantial thud, then carried her coffee to her.

"French vanilla, with one sugar," he said as he eased the metal cup out of the carrier and set it down next to her.

"Excellent. Thank you. What did you get yourself this morning?"

"Something… raspberry… mocha. I'll probably lapse into a coma before 7:00 a.m. with all the sugar I poured into mine."

"Well, I'll revive you if need be. I did that whole CPR training thing at the, oh, what was that? Where was I?"

"Bond Traders' Convention in Reno?"

"Yes!"

"With the showgirls dressed like accrued interest with those blue chips…"

"Right again!"

"Oh, well, I feel completely safe then. Bond traders and CPR go hand in hand," he said facetiously.

She rose from the computer console, made her way over to her desk and started going through the bundles. Paul Peter sat in the chair opposite her, waiting for any instructions while he sipped his sugary drink.

"Hmm...what's this?" she murmured to herself as she perused the bundles.

Using a special cutting tool, she opened the bundle and pulled a small, handwritten note from inside.

Paul Peter eyed her with amusement as she turned the envelope over and over in her hands before breaking the seal and sliding the card out. She smiled softly to herself as she read the note.

"From our mysterious Mr. Shanks?" Paul asked her.

"Yes, another thank-you note."

She showed him the front of the card that displayed a little gray kitten playing with a ball of red yarn. The yarn had looped comically over the kitten's ears, and an artist had airbrushed highlights into the eyes, making them look bigger and more vulnerable.

Paul Peter doubled over, laughing hysterically.

"A kitten? Where does this guy shop? His grandmother's panty drawer?"

"I think it's sweet."

"A thank-you note, after, how much money did you make for him just last week?"

"Seven hundred thousand."

"Uh-huh. That rates, what, a Porsche at least?"

"No, I don't think so," she laughed.

"Well, he can buy one for me. I love German engineering. I'd even play with a ball of yarn for one. No, seriously, I would. Wouldn't even have to be mohair; I'd go acrylic."

"Where are your standards?" she joked with him as she opened a drawer in her desk and set the note in there on top of other cards with similar, sugary themes. Digging further into the courier pouch, she started pulling out wrapped bundles of cash, which Paul Peter stacked up on her desk as he counted them.

"Fifty thousand," he added up the final tally.

"Wow."

"Must be some coffee can he's got buried in the backyard."

"At least!"

"Chock full o' tens and twenties and trillion-dollar bills!"

Her phone started to ring, and Paul Peter let it hit two and a half chimes before he picked it up.

"Amanda Brax's office," he answered, then after a beat, said, "yes sir, one moment. I'll put her on directly."

Paul Peter held the receiver out to her while he wiggled his eyebrows suggestively.

"Him?" she whispered.

"Herr Shanks. Yes."

Amanda took the phone from him.

"This is Amanda."

Paul Peter squinted as the sun's rays started to pierce the room. While she spoke, he went over to the blinds and adjusted them against the glare.

"My goodness Mr. Shanks, it must be the wee hours of the night. Are you still in Germany?"

Villicus spoke to her across the miles on a sleek black and chrome cell phone. He had located a phone store open late one night in Berlin and spoke for over an hour with the sales clerk, learning how to operate the elegant device, selecting a service and most importantly, picking out the song that would play whenever his phone rang should he get to know someone who might think to call him. Villicus went with a Country and Western tune made famous by the Judds. The sales clerk had joked with him about the vibration feature, saying that most men liked to leave it on, deep in their pants pockets, for when their girlfriends called them. Villicus did not get the joke and bashed the clerk's head in with a floor display for crush-proof cell phone covers.

He held the phone lightly against his ear while he brushed a few specks of plaster from his expensive and exquisitely cut black jacket. He looked amazing in his beautiful clothes and his pearly gray skin, glowing with perfect Vampire health. Villicus was calling her from an office that had recently been tossed. Smashed furniture lay in piles around his feet, and pictures hung at severe angles on the walls.

He moved across the room, pushing debris out of his way. A soft moaning sound at his feet caused him to look down. He watched Jonah Leeks, the manager of the Krause Sternberg

Bank & Trust of Heidelberg whose offices Villicus had just trashed, crawling along the ground. Jonah's face was bloodied and battered, his breath whistling through gaps in his teeth where Villicus had knocked them out. Jonah saw Villicus's foot, clad in incredibly expensive boots, standing next to his face, and he cried out in fear as he struggled to crawl under the debris. Villicus smiled sweetly down at him.

"Yes. I'm in Heidelberg. Did you get my package?" Villicus continued his conversation with Amanda.

"Got it. All $50,000."

"Good. That's amazing to me. You see, I just sent it yesterday."

The man at Villicus's feet, seeing the phone, moaned a bit louder, hoping to God someone might hear. Vampire-quick, Villicus knelt down and clamped his hand over Jonah's mouth, shutting him up as he rammed his head painfully hard into what was left of his office chair.

"Mr. Shanks…"

"Villicus. Please Amanda, call me Villicus. I insist," he said amicably.

"Very well then, Villicus, did you want me to deposit this cash into an interest-bearing account for you until I can select a stock…?"

"No, thank you, no, I have already selected the stock. A company called Schwermut."

"Oh," Amanda sounded a bit surprised. Villicus had usually trusted her to make any decisions regarding stock purchases. This was the first time he had actually requested a specific acquisition.

"Schwermut. Okay, let me get to my computer," she said.

"Take your time," Villicus said as he choked off Jonah's air supply until he fainted, then lightly slapped the man on the face, reviving him again.

Villicus heard Amanda making her way over to her computers while he kept up his morbid little game on his side of the world.

"Alright," Amanda said, with the audible ding of her opening stock-purchase program. "Schwermut, hmmmm, Schwermut."

"Oh, okay, here it is," Amanda said triumphantly.

She opened up a fact page about the company but did not seem all that happy with what she read.

"Hmm, it's just a holding company based here in Los Angeles. Seems it used to be, oh, right there in Heidelberg."

"Yes, I know. It took me some time to locate them, but I finally ran across one of their financial officers. I had to persuade him to give me the information, but he was finally happy to give it to me."

Villicus smiled at the bank manager, then cracked another tooth out of his jaw.

"Oh, that was nice of him. You know, we do a lot of cash transactions here, but it's unusual to get so many from one client."

Villicus rose and moved across the demolished office, noticing one painting he had left on the wall. He flipped it out of his way with ease. A small, but strong safe was buried in the plaster and lathe behind it. Villicus studied it for a moment, then snapped the lock off and ripped the door from its hinges. Inside were stacks of money, which he quickly grabbed and tossed into a small bag on a nearby table.

"I prefer cash. Just a quirk of mine."

"No problem. Okay, you want to invest the full $50,000 in this company?"

Villicus looked at a couple of bundles of cash in his hand.

"Yes," he said. "And you can expect another shipment of cash from me. When you receive that, I'd like you to buy into the same company."

"Okay, you got it. I don't think you're going to make much of a profit with this investment, though. You'd need to hold the stocks for a long time."

"Time is not an issue for me. Please, invest all of it."

"Fine. Consider it done."

He heard the keystrokes as Amanda entered the information, then hit the execute button.

"Okay," she went on. "It's a done deal."

"I knew I could count on you. Oh, and Amanda, just one more thing."

"Yes?"

"I'll be coming to Los Angeles soon, to see to my investments personally. I will look forward to meeting you, if I may?"

Villicus tossed the last bit of cash into the bag and zipped it closed. He retrieved an expensive flask from next to the bag, opened it then recoiled from the aroma emanating from the neck of the bottle. He tossed the contents of the bottle onto Jonah, who was more dead than alive, lying in a pool of his own blood. Villicus cast the empty flask into the corner, then quickly lit a lighter and tossed that onto Jonah, who abruptly erupted into a ball of flame. The man writhed on the floor as he burned alive.

"Oh, of course," Amanda said cheerfully. "And likewise. I really look forward to meeting you as well."

Villicus picked up the bag of cash, then calmly walked away from the small inferno.

"Guten Abend, Amanda," Villicus said just before he terminated the call.

After Amanda hung up the phone, she double-checked to make sure the purchase order went through.

"What the hell do you know that I don't, Herr Shanks," she whispered to herself.

Paul Peter had moved out to his office area, then returned with a small plastic container that he started to scoop the money into.

"To the vault with this?" he asked.

"Yup. Transaction complete."

"That was fast."

"Well, he knew what he wanted."

Paul Peter gathered up the last of the bundles of cash.

"I'll just trot this down to my car...the vault!" he kidded.

"You know you will," Amanda chided him.

She wrote her transaction down in a log, then noticed her monitors start to flutter.

"Uh oh," she moaned.

"What? What's up?"

Paul Peter came to stand behind her, holding the container of money like it was a basket of laundry. He and Amanda watched her monitors flicker from the digital readouts of the financial markets she had been tracking to the Delancey logo and then their flashing Security Lockdown image.

"Damn! What's going on?"

Her phone rang, and Paul Peter quickly ran to answer it.

"Ms. Brax's office, uh huh, yes, do you want me to get her? Okay. I'll let her know immediately."

"What's up?"

"That was Mr. Hogan's office."

"Oh yeah, our fearless security guy."

"They've shut the system down."

"No kidding. Did anyone say why?"

"We've been hacked."

Amanda and Paul Peter exchanged a worried glance.

"Not a good way to start the morning," Paul Peter observed.

"No, it doesn't get much worse than that," Amanda agreed with him.

As the sun continued its climb over the rising city of the angels, more and more people spilled out onto the downtown streets. Los Angeles, being a warm city year-round, had more than its share of homeless people. They made small communities under the bridges and overpasses and in the stairwells of the meager subway system.

Patsy Honeywell, just seventeen but homeless for over a year now, started her morning routine, moving through the alleys near the expensive restaurants to investigate the dumpsters. Close to MacPeak's, the newest hot spot to visit, she pulled an old wooden crate along behind her to step up and have a look inside the huge garbage containers.

She found part of a pressed duck dinner, two bags of three-day-old rolls and the body of a woman with her throat torn out.

Chapter Four

Homicide Detective Kim Barnstall, steadfast and focused, strode down the hallway of the police headquarters where she worked with her younger but not inexperienced partner, James Montgomery. She wore a nicely cut linen jacket, coral in color, that was set off by her understated but stylish ivory slacks and simple blouse. Her dark hair was fashioned into short dreadlocks that bounced lightly as her shoes tapped along on the old green and gray linoleum.

Without looking up, Kim snapped one eight by ten color photo after another out of a standard manila folder and held each one up in front of her, studying the image. Her coworkers flowed around her, gracefully and with practiced ease, as she forged her way down the well-worn hall.

Turning smartly to the right, she entered the detectives' room, jammed with cops, old wooden desks and moldy coffee cups. Dozens of boxes were stacked against the far wall, filled with active cases. Homicide was working overtime lately, and their cases had long since overflowed from the jammed metal filing cabinets squeezed in between the filthy windows.

James, boyish looking and blonde, was making room on a corkboard wall filled with photos of murder victims. The people in the photos did not bear any close resemblance to each other, with one exception—they all had similar fatal, grotesque throat wounds.

James watched Kim approach.

"Maria Dolores Ramirez, twenty-eight, employed at the Red Rooster all-night café, worked until approximately 2 o'clock this morning when some asshole did this to her," Kim said as she continued to study the photos.

Kim handed James a photo of Maria Dolores Ramirez, a once pretty young woman now looking gray, disheveled and very dead with matted hair and huge blotches staining her skin from the blood and garbage she had been laying in. Her throat bore a similar wound to the other victims pictured on the wall.

"That makes eight in three weeks." James noted.

"Exactly. Some fool has a real taste for this kind of killing, no pun intended."

"Preliminary forensics?"

"They're coming up with a lot of the same stuff. No saliva in the wound. Appears to have been torn by teeth or fangs. Not any animal they are familiar with, but the bridge width matches that of an average adult male."

"Total absence of saliva?"

"Yup. Go figure."

"See!" James interjected. "It's some kind of fucked up weapon or some guy wearing like this full mouth prosthetic."

James pantomimed shoving a prosthetic in his wide-open mouth.

"I'd buy that too, except the coroner keeps bringing us away from that because," Kim points to one of the throat wounds where the skin has been ripped open, "a human jaw isn't strong enough to do that."

James studied the photo for a moment, examining the gruesome tear that had pulled open the throat all the way to the spinal column.

"Maybe yes, maybe no. What about some jerk on PCP, or some new pharmaceutical?"

"Yeah, well, that might be."

"Sexual assault?"

"Preliminary says no, but she was like Mrs. Hershman and Jane Doe #7 over there," Kim pointed to the photos. "Lots of vaginal secretions."

"She was sexually aroused at time of death?"

"Seems so. Oh, and we got that other weird thing too."

"No blood?"

"Most of it gone, yes, and not enough pooled around the body to indicate she bled out there and no evidence of blood anywhere in the area signifying Maria Dolores Ramirez was carried there. She apparently died right where she was found."

James and Kim stared at the sordid collection of photos for a while, and then he finally asked no one in particular, "We talking Dracula here?"

Amanda hustled into the largest windowed meeting room at Delancey. She scanned the room quickly, efficiently, noting all the traders and brokers crammed in the space. As she made her way across the room, delicately squeezing into a chair jammed between a tall potted plant and an enormous TV monitor used for satellite conferencing, she thought about the talent represented here. Delancey was one of the biggest financial institutions in the world, and it still amazed her that she was part of this huge, well-oiled, money-making machine.

A slight disturbance near the door she just came through caused her to look up. With some disgust, she noticed Mark Hadley, another trader, five years her senior in the company, fighting his way through the crowd to roll a chair over by her.

"Excuse me. Coming through. Hey, thanks a bunch. You're my best buddy," he said with little charm as he rolled the chair over people's toes and banged it into their knees.

The other people crowded around Amanda were happy to move out of Hadley's way. If he had not been one of the top producers in the company, most assumed he would have been found dead in an alley somewhere, bludgeoned to death with *Standard and Poor's Midcap Index*. He rolled his chair closer and whispered in a conspiratorial tone to her.

"Hey, Sunshine? What's up? Why the emergency meeting?"

Disgusted, she could feel spray from his saliva brush across her throat.

"I guess we'll find out, won't we," Amanda said, doing her best to look past the plant she was pushed up against to stare out the window. She noted with some interest a strange stain on the window that looked slightly like the country of Panama. She wished she were in Panama at that very moment.

Hadley leaned over and whispered to her, gently caressing her arm as he did so.

"Come on, Mandy, you know everything."

"It's Amanda. Usually I do, but this time, I am in the dark, just like you."

Amanda pulled her arm away from him, noting with some delight that he did not get her barb. She had known him for three years now, ever since she came to Delancey, and she knew he would get it, about an hour later, and then take it out on some poor secretary. She hoped it would be Paul Peter, because he was much better at the subtle slams than she was.

Before Hadley could molest her any further, the president of Delancey, J. Richmond Gaines, strode into the room accompanied by Blake Hogan, the firm's head of security.

"Good morning, people," Richmond said affably. "Thank you all for dropping what you were doing and meeting here so quickly."

"It's not like we could do any work, ya' twit," Hadley whispered snidely.

"What's happened?" one of the brokers asked.

"Is it true? We were hacked?" another asked loudly.

"Yes," Richmond and Blake said together.

"You take it from here, Blake. Fill them in if you would."

Richmond stepped aside, letting the ruffled looking Blake address everyone from the head of the table.

"Sometime after midnight," Blake went on, "a pirate hacked into the system through a telephone line that was not widely used."

"Where? Where was this line?" another trader piped up.

"Well," Blake sounded downright embarrassed now, "the executive men's room."

There was a stunned silence followed by a wave of cautious laughter.

"Man, can't even take a piss anymore," Hadley hissed.

A few traders around him giggled nervously.

Blake went on.

"The hacker was able to tap into the line, which is hooked to the others here by way of the intercom. It took a lot of perseverance, someone with a lot of time on their hands. We've shut down access to the system over all lines for now. We're also installing new phones today that are closed, just for internal use. This will eliminate any possible hacking like this in the future."

"Sneaky little bastard," Hadley added.

"Was any data stolen? Money, stocks, anything?" asked one of the brokers.

"Any of the accounts altered?" another asked.

"No, thank God," Richmond chimed in. "All of the material has been re-encrypted and checked against yesterday's volumes. No data was altered. Just some joker having a look at what we got. Probably didn't even know what they were looking at."

Blake filled them in on more of the safety features being installed and ways they could prevent any more infiltration of their systems, then the meeting broke up. Brokers and traders hustled back to their offices, waiting anxiously to get back into their accounts. Outside the conference room door, Richmond waved Amanda over.

"Amanda, I know you've had a lot of overseas activity that's being filed in our blind accounts…"

"Yes, I'm really worried about this situation," she cut him off. "We've got a lot of high-profile clients who depend on us to protect their confidentiality."

"I've asked Hogan to give your accounts priority. You've been bringing a lot of business to us lately, a lot of business. I just wanted you to know we're really pleased with the production, and we've got our eye on you."

"Thank you, J. I appreciate that."

"Keep up the good work." Richmond shook her hand before he wandered off down the hallway to his huge corner office.

Amanda caught Mark Hadley out of the corner of her eye, struggling to get through the crowd of financial wizards, looking every bit like a salmon fighting to get upstream. She felt trapped and began to hurry down the hallway, trying to get back to her office before he could catch her.

"Mandy! Wait up!" Hadley called after her.

She continued to stride down the hallway. At the very least, she could make it to the ladies' room on the corner and take sanctuary in there, but he caught her, latching squarely onto her elbow.

"Whoa, Mandy, what's the rush?"

"I have work to do, don't you?"

"What work? The system will be down for a while."

"I do have things to do that don't require my computers."

"Plans for later? Get some dinner with me, maybe? We could head down to the Sunset Club, have a few drinks…you know, whatever…"

"Oh! Whatever! Sorry, but I can't do whatever tonight. You have fun though," she said as she shook loose from him and continued down the hallway, muttering under her breath. "Yes, you have fun. You can pick up a date or two on the way, at any street corner."

"Okay, another time then sweetie," Hadley called after her.

She could see Hadley's reflection in the window of one of the offices she passed by and noticed he was staring squarely at her ass. She bit her lip hard, fighting the urge to turn around, walk back to him and slap the lascivious look from his face.

Rounding the last corner, she flew into her office, past a startled Paul Peter who sat there with one finger in the air. Unsuccessful at getting her attention, he jumped up and ran in after her, carrying a memo.

"Was it that bad? What happened? Did someone get fired? Oh, no! Did I get fired!" he blurted out, trying to joke with her.

Amanda had slammed herself down into her chair, one heel of her expensive, black boot jammed into the rug to anchor her as she pivoted angrily back and forth.

She worked hard to maintain a stone face as she stared at Paul Peter, whose lower lip was now quivering comically. Unable to maintain any longer, Amanda doubled over laughing in loud, gun-blast bursts. The absurdity of the entire morning was too much, what with Hadley, the situation with the executive men's room, getting hacked–all of it.

Gulping air between sentences, she managed to relay all the information to Paul Peter who descended elegantly into the chair across from her, perched on the edge as he listened intently to what she had to say.

"The executive men's room," he said laconically. "Well, we know it wasn't me, because although I think highly of myself, I'm not an executive. And, unless you are really hiding something, we know it wasn't you. I'm really not surprised, though. The urinals, you knew they were hi-tech listening devices, didn't you? It's the cakes they put in there."

"Oh my God," Amanda said, still gasping for air from laughing. "If this ever leaks out..."

Amanda and Paul Peter locked eyes for a split second.

"Leaks," they shrieked together.

After another round of cleansing laughter, Amanda finally leaned back, wiping a few tears from the corners of her eyes.

Paul flipped his hand around so the memo he had been holding stood straight up in the air. He stared in a nonchalant way at it.

Amanda started to stare at it too.

"What is that?" she asked.

"What is what?" he snapped the comment back at her.

"That, in your hand there."

Paul Peter relaxed his fingers slightly, so the paper folded over on itself, looking like a sleeping bird. He opened and closed his other hand, waggling his fingers at her.

"Nothing, see? I don't have anything in my hand."

"You had better give it to me, or I'm going to have to hurt you."

"Well, alright," he said, sounding wounded, playing the moment for all he could.

He picked a pink marker pen from the jar on her desk and drew several arrows on the memo pointing at the one line of copy before he laid it down reverently in front of her.

The one line of copy read, *Villicus Shanks arriving at Burbank Airport, 11p.m., private jet.*

"Tonight!" Amanda gasped.

"Ya vol. But that's not all."

"What else?"

"He wants to know if you are available to pick him up."

Amanda sat back, blinking her eyes at him. Paul Peter,

without giving her a moment to respond, continued.

"I told him yes, you would, and I reserved the company limo for you. Do you think his jet will have a cute little kitten painted on the side? God, I hope so."

Later that evening, Amanda sat in the back of the limo, struggling with a German phrase book as she waited for Villicus's jet to arrive.

"Wie get...geht es...Ihneb. Wie geht es Ihneb," she fumbled with the words. "How are you? Oh geez, this sucks! I suck! How in the hell do German people ever learn to speak this way?"

She leafed through the book a bit more, picking a phrase out at random.

"Ich werde einen Hut kaufen. I am going to buy a hat. A hat! What do I need to know that for? Wow, I'm going to impress the lederhosen right off of this guy."

The driver of the limo tapped on the window separating the front from the back before he lowered the glass.

"They're taxiing in right now," he said.

"Oh, great. Thanks."

Amanda started to ditch the book but thought better of it. She stepped out onto the tarmac and watched the sleek Gulfstream roll to a stop just a few feet from her limo. The door quickly opened as soon as the turbines began their final whine, and an attendant jumped out.

"Is he, err...is Mr. Shanks on board?" Amanda asked the attendant.

"Oh yes, he'll be right out," the attendant answered with a thick German accent.

"I'll bet he's exhausted. You flew straight in from Munich, didn't you?"

"Yes, we did. Well, we cleared customs in New York, but he slept almost all the way from Germany. We barely saw him. He kept to his room in the back most of the flight."

Amanda had her back to the doorway of the jet as she talked to the attendant directing the luggage being offloaded to the trunk of the limo.

Noticing the attendant looking up and over her shoulder,

Amanda spun around and saw Villicus directly in front of her, smiling. His exotic looks and powerful presence were potent, hypnotic. She could not take her eyes off him.

The phrase book hung uselessly in her hands.

"Amanda?" he asked gently.

She nodded dumbly.

Taking her hand in his, he kissed it lightly, noticing the phrase book.

"Ich bin sehr erfreut Sie endlich kennenzulernen," he whispered to her.

"Wha...t?" she stammered back.

He tugged the book from her hand and leafed through it until he found an appropriate page.

"I said, 'I'm so pleased to finally meet you.' And you would reply..."

He held the book up so she could see the page with the usual response. Without reading it, she playfully pulled the book from his hands.

"Likewise!" she laughed.

Villicus smiled at the joke, enjoying her spirit.

"Shall we go?" he asked, noticing his bags were all in the trunk.

He escorted her to the limo and followed her inside.

"Your hotel? Can we take you there...first?" she asked.

Villicus smiled at the stammering way in which she was speaking to him.

"No, no hotel," he said. "Let's go to my home."

"Your home?" Amanda asked, quite surprised.

"Yes, I bought one here a few weeks ago."

Villicus gave the address to the driver, and they sped off into the LA night.

They headed down the freeway towards downtown Los Angeles. Villicus stared out of the windows of the car like an amazed child. The sights of the city fascinated him. They passed beneath the enormous Hollywood sign, standing vigil over the city since the 1920s.

Amanda watched him, both fascinated and amused by his behavior, as he sounded the name "Hollywood" out loud.

"What is that?" he asked her.

"Oh, it's a famous landmark here. Hollywood is where the movies get made."

Villicus gazed back up at the sign.

"Is it for sale?"

Amanda laughed at first, then realized he was serious.

"I don't know. I'll find out for you."

Realizing he was new to Los Angeles, Amanda instructed the driver to exit the freeway earlier than their turnoff so they could drive through Hollywood. Villicus watched in amazement the colorful panoply of people wandering up and down Sunset Blvd. Passing the Viper Room, he noticed a line of people gathered outside, most dressed in black leather and a vast array of wildly colored hair.

"I like this place already," he said, his face literally pressed up against the glass.

"I'm glad," Amanda said, studying his every nuance.

A few minutes later, they were pulling in through the gated entrance to the high-rise where Villicus had purchased his condo. Once the car had stopped, Villicus immediately opened the door and exited, pulling Amanda along with him.

"You will accompany me, please."

It sounded more like an order than a request, but Amanda was happy to oblige. She did not want to abandon his presence just yet, not to mention the fact he was her wealthiest client.

Together they strode into the lavish lobby. Villicus headed immediately towards the concierge and a small group of security people gathered behind a counter.

"Herr Shanks?" the concierge asked.

Villicus nodded.

The concierge pulled some items out from below the counter and set them down for Villicus.

"Yes, sir. Good to have you with us. Here are the keys to your home, and Devonshire Motors delivered your car this morning. It's parked in space 19A under the building. Also, Cross Systems was in your home earlier this week, installing the security cameras and additional monitors you requested. All under my supervision of course, as per your specific instructions."

"Of course," Villicus said, pleased with the service so far.

The concierge explained to Villicus how the fob for his car keys had an electronic code to open the big mesh doorway covering the entrance to the underground parking area. All he had to do was drive towards the door. The fob would do the rest.

Villicus gathered up his belongings and, taking Amanda by the hand, strode toward the elevators. One of the security people had already run ahead and was holding the doors open. Villicus and Amanda stepped inside, letting the doors sweep shut. He studied the panel for a bit, not pressing any of the buttons.

"Do you know which floor?" Amanda asked.

"Yes. The top."

He pressed the topmost button and frowned deeply when nothing happened.

"Oh, your key," Amanda suggested.

"What?"

She teased a key from his hand and inserted it into the panel, turning it to the right. The top light on the panel immediately lit up, and the car began to rise swiftly. She handed the key back to him.

"Thank you, Amanda," he said, taking the key from her.

Once the car had risen all the way to the top, the doors opened into the private foyer of his home. The hallway was deep, large enough for sofas, chairs and a stunning table covered in a casual but brilliant display of multicolored roses and pears. Narrow slit windows graced the top of the wall, and as they made their way to the double doors, Amanda could just make out the moon peeking through.

Villicus easily negotiated the front doors and swung them both open, stepping into the living room. On the other side of the door was a small hardwood stage-like area with three steps that went down into the enormous living room, sporting the largest blue and cream Oriental rug Amanda had ever seen.

Then again, Amanda had never seen a penthouse quite like this one before. Villicus walked through the huge room toward the massive two-story window looking out over the Hollywood

Hills. The lights in the hills twinkled in the night, backlit beautifully by the enormous, honey moon.

She came up behind him.

"Do you like it?" he asked.

"It's amazing!"

"Yes, I think so, too. It is."

He stopped to stare up into the ceiling which was covered over by an enormous neon sculpture of the sun. Looking about, Amanda located a switch by the door and flipped them each on until the sun started to light up. The effect was stunning, and not in the least overwhelming, from such a huge sculpture. All the light was cast up into the ceiling, so it was reflected back down onto them as a gentle glow. As the gases warmed, it became clear that the sculpture was somewhat kinetic. The light subtly glowed then dimmed as the gasses expanded and moved through the intricate network of glass tubes.

"That is incredible!"

"Do you like it?"

"Oh yes! This came with the penthouse?"

"No. I bought it at the Biennale in Venice a few weeks ago."

"That was shipped here from Venice?"

He nodded then walked back through the room again, followed by Amanda. A few pieces of furniture dotted the room. Some very old-fashioned, probably centuries old, and shipped over here by Villicus. They actually fit in very well with the new, ultra-modern pieces in the room.

Several large wooden crates were scattered about as well. He spotted one that caught his attention and with a flick of his hand, snapped the top off. Amanda gasped at this display of strength but did not say anything.

He pulled the front of the crate away with equal ease, then quickly emptied it of the shipping straw. Amanda laughed when she saw the bizarre pinball machine inside. Villicus frowned at her laughter but continued with what he was doing. He located the power cord and nearby outlet, then plugged it in. The machine whirred to life, making loud dinging sounds and flashing brightly.

The pinball game was played with funny wheeled bobsleds

racing down a snow-covered mountain rather than the usual pinballs. He activated a lever and launched several of the silly, brightly colored sleds up the mountain and then kept them up on the mountain by using levers that caused pine trees, snowbanks, rocks and mountain goats to swoop about, hitting them back to the top.

Villicus laughed loudly as he played the game with Amanda standing to one side, marveling at his childlike demeanor. She looked about and noticed that his movers, or the concierge most likely, had opened more of the crates. There were dozens of other electronic games, several computers, TV monitors and expensive sound systems. The operative word of everything she saw was *expensive*.

Turning back to him, she asked, "Is that your favorite?"

"Just a toy," he said, still playing the game. "I like to collect toys. What do you like to collect?"

"Oh, clients, I suppose."

"You like your work, the money, the power?"

"And the interesting people I get to meet."

Villicus stopped playing the game, turning to face her, resting his hypnotic gaze on her.

She flinched slightly and took a step backward, but he quickly caught her hand and kept her from moving.

"You seem frightened," he said.

"No, not at all," she stammered.

He smiled and released her, then started to move through the room again. Amanda followed him only with her eyes this time until a large metallic object caught her attention from across the room. She moved towards it, this time feeling Villicus eyes following her.

She came up to the metal object and saw that it was an enormous cross, perhaps five feet tall, poking part way out of its crate. The object was obviously very old but beautiful, made of bronze with silver and gold details.

"This is amazing," she said, letting her fingers trail delicately along the top edge.

Villicus came to stand next to her.

"Is it?"

"Yes, it's a stunning piece. I had no idea you were such an avid art collector."

"You think of this as art?"

"Oh yes, don't you? Where did you get it?"

"St. Bartholoma's church, just outside of Stuttgart."

"Oh? Did you belong to this church? An altar boy perhaps?"

He smiled wryly at her joke.

"No, but I did spend a lot of time there. Come with me." He took her hand again and headed to a chrome and glass spiral staircase.

"Where are you taking me?" she asked, holding back slightly, somewhat afraid.

"Not to worry, Amanda."

He tugged her along gently behind him, up to a stunning second-floor hallway carpeted in a deep green pile that set off the maple walls beautifully. He moved along the hallway until he arrived at a glass door and then led her out onto the roof.

"Oh!" she said, sounding very relieved. "It's beautiful up here. Wow, what a view you have."

They moved through a tiled courtyard landscaped with huge potted trees, bougainvillea, jasmine and ivy, past the blue and white hot tub and the inevitable wet bar.

Villicus walked out to the edge of the roof and without even hesitating, stepped up onto the ledge, his toes hanging off. He spread his arms out like an eagle and stared towards the Hollywood Hills.

Watching this, Amanda could feel her knees start to buckle from fear. What did he think he was doing?

"Villicus. Villicus! Oh my God! What are you doing?"

"I'm enjoying the view."

"Please, come down, please. You're scaring me."

"Don't be scared, Amanda, not of me or anything that I do."

He turned and looked down at her, observing the terror in her face. He stepped down and moved toward her, taking her face in his hands.

"I'm sorry I frightened you."

"It's alright, I...it's just..."

"I want you to know," he went on, sliding his hands from her face, "how grateful I am for your services. Due to circumstances beyond my control, my fortune was lost. You have helped me to get it back."

He removed a small jewelry case from inside his jacket pocket, opened it and toyed with something inside with his pinky finger. Satisfied, he turned it around so she could see the necklace inside.

"What is this?"

"A small token of my gratitude?"

"It's not a kitten?" she stammered.

"What?"

"Oh, no…nothing."

She could barely hide her embarrassment, but the moment had already passed for Villicus. She liked that about him. He moved fluidly from one instant to the next, without looking back.

Taking the necklace from the box, he stood behind her and fastened it about her neck. She looked down, gently cradling the pendant, and noticed how the moonlight was captured in the stunning diamond.

Overwhelmed perhaps by the moment of sheer terror she had felt when he stood poised on the edge of death a few moments ago, or the beauty of the gem, or seeing the sun glowing from inside his home, she turned and slipped her arms up and around his neck and kissed him gently.

He did not turn away, nor did he return the kiss. His arms remained at his side.

Puzzled, she backed away from him, staring up into his amazing blue eyes.

"I'm so sorry…I misread…"

"Nothing to be sorry for, Amanda," he said, gently pressing his finger against her lips.

A few moments later Villicus was back inside, turning on the security monitors that Cross Systems had installed for him. He had a three-hundred-and-sixty-degree view from his home and watched Amanda walk toward the limo downstairs. He studied her on several monitors as she stopped and looked back up to the top of the building, again cradling the jewel in her fingers that now hung suspended from her perfect, ivory neck.

Chapter Five

"Open up. Fucker!"

Bale, tracking worldwide financial markets from the coziness of his office, looked over at the security monitor showing the image from his front door.

There was Nikonar, staring angrily up at the camera, clutching a small, frilly looking shopping bag in one hand and flipping him the bird with the other. Bale laughed at the outrageous behavior of this young vampire.

The elaborate computer system Bale possessed spoke to him.

"You have a visitor at the main door. It is Nikonar Federov," the melodic computerized voice spoke.

"Thank you," Bale responded as he keyed a password into his security computer system. His front door popped open and Bale watched as Nikonar casually sauntered through, then the door closed and locked itself behind him.

Bale tracked Nikonar's movements through the massive house on his many monitors, watching the vampire move effortlessly through dark as well as lit rooms. Nikonar passed through the darkened dining room, then stopped in the hallway outside and returned. Bale had recently renovated the room in a style reminiscent of the era when the house was built, the 1920s—when Hollywood was awash with starlets, new money and loose morals. That was exactly the kind of crowd Bale loved to associate with.

He watched Nikonar play with the lighting scheme, noticing how the wiring suspended from a system of cables mounted on the wall moved tiny lights back and forth behind a beautifully painted scrim of a blue dragon flying through a burst of flame. The lights made the fire appear as if it were consuming the dragon who ultimately made it through unscathed, appearing whole once again.

The furniture, beautifully restored and upholstered in delicate peach and cream velvet, looked like it hovered over the heavily patterned early Chinese rug woven in shades of deep blue, golden brown and cream.

The walls were covered with black and white photos of Victorian angels, contemporary rock stars and divas from the twenties, all framed in different colors of glowing neon. A spectacular sculpture made up of thousands of strands of tiny pearls hung from the ceiling, suspended from a grid of purple, silver and metallic green glass filaments and lit by small halogen lamps. It swayed and turned very gently in the light breeze caused when Nikonar passed through the room. The effect of the lights bouncing around, back and forth, inside the sculpture itself was breathtaking.

Nikonar walked about the room, running his fingertips over the sumptuous surfaces. Poised delicately in the center of the dining room table was an elaborate, tiny antique water clock balanced with exquisite shells and semi-precious stones, all of an aqua hue to imitate water. In the corner of the room, a floor to ceiling aquarium was home to fabulously expensive koi in colors that matched or complimented the décor. Even the thick, pure white sand covering the expansive bottom of the tank was raked and arranged just so. Bale did like to control every aspect of his environment.

Nikonar left the room, leaving all the lights blazing, and continued moving through the rest of the house. Bale could hear him approach now, his boots clicking confidently on the pegged, ancient wooden floor that had come from the Borgia's home estate in Italy.

Nikonar appeared in the doorway of Bale's office, his six-foot-seven frame completely filling the space. Dangling from Nikonar's hand was the small gift bag topped off with a puff of pink and gold decorative tissue paper to keep the treasure hidden inside. The petite, delicate gift seemed comical hanging from the Russian's enormous hand.

"Hello, Bale," Nikonar said, a slight trace of his Russian heritage still coloring his pronunciation. "Having fun?"

"Yes, always. And you?"

"Absolutely. Look, I brought you a present."

Nikonar held the bag out to him, draped off of one finger.

"Oh? What is it?"

"Come on! Look and see. I picked it out myself."

Nikonar handed the bag to Bale who, with a flourish, plucked the tissue into the air and let it drift off where it settled delicately on the floor. He reached inside and drew out a small but heavy stone statue. He rotated it around in his hands until the hideous face of the malevolent South American god Colo-Colo stared up at him.

"I thought of you immediately when I saw it," Nikonar chirped at him.

"Yes, I can see why. It's really something."

Nikonar burst out laughing, enjoying his little joke. Bale smiled and ran his fingers over the maw of the hideous creature, feeling the teeth and protruding tongue. It was quite gruesome, and Bale loved it.

"So, what have I missed?" Nikonar asked.

"Oh, come with me. I'll fill you in."

Bale rose and tucked the statue under his arm, then slid past Nikonar into the hallway. The two vampires walked through the house.

"Did you like my new dining room?" Bale asked pleasantly.

"It's amazing. You really outdid yourself this time."

"Oh? You think so?"

"Yes, completely. Fascinating photos and the furniture! That rug! And what on earth is that amazing light sculpture hanging from the ceiling! Astounding. Although, why you spend so much time and money on a room for eating when you yourself do not eat, nor will anyone actually ever eat anything in there, well, it's beyond me."

"It amuses me."

"Of course it does."

The two reached the largest room in the house, the living

room, built like a huge box car some one hundred and twenty by eighty feet.

"Lights!" Bale cried out.

The room lit up, his voice activating the computer governing the elaborate indirect lighting system. Nikonar followed him into the room and dropped heavily into a large armchair near the truck-sized fireplace. The room was almost frightening to be in, it was so expensively and outrageously decorated. The floor was made up of several materials—ancient timbers of polished ebony that came from Babylon itself nestled next to chunks of marble taken from Nero's own palace. There were even a few fascinating burn marks in the sumptuous stone.

Dovetailed neatly with the marble were bricks from the Tower of London, still showing axe marks and stains, and so on. The sections of flooring continued in this fashion—wood, stone, hand painted porcelain tiles, bricks and glass medallions, all brought from famous, infamous and ancient homes throughout the world. Each and every piece had at one time in history been splattered with human blood. Bale had indeed shopped carefully.

To tie them together, Bale had strips of Lucite poured between them. He embedded it with actual coins from throughout the centuries, dozens of currencies from different countries and cultures, lit from inside with fiber optic lights. The massively heavy floor seemed to hover due to the glowing effects.

The walls were covered with enormous, original tapestries, oil paintings and sculptures, many ripped from churches, museums or private homes. Whatever Bale fancied, he helped himself to. Usually, though, he preferred to buy these things. He adored spending vast quantities of cash, just to see the human salesman grovel and scrape as the deal was finalized.

Then more often than not, Bale would return to that same salesman later, in the dead of night, and allow the human to try to barter for his life. Bale would stand, poised in some impossible place for a human to be—perched elegantly on the head of a newel post or standing gracefully along the top edge of a framed painting—so he could look down on the human gibbering and slipping into shock, knowing their fate was sealed as he toyed with them.

"What price for your life?" Bale would hiss at them, running his fingers along their temple, then down their jaw to poke the jugular vein and watch the blood thump just under the surface of the sweating, taut skin.

They would offer anything, even their own children, to escape this hideous death he offered them. This game would go on for hours and hours until the human was on the verge of suicide, and then Bale would strike, vampire-fast, grasping his prey in his hands, powerful enough to pull a human head from its shoulders. And Bale, master at taking life, made the event drag itself out, relishing in the fear he inflicted. In the end, he always got what he wanted. Some new, fabulous work of art or piece of furniture and a belly full of warm, human blood.

Bale placed the statue of Colo Colo up on the mantle where it sat by itself, just off center, below an original twelfth-century Giotto of the Madonna and Child that no one had ever seen since Bale had taken it from the artist himself centuries ago.

"Perfect!" Nikonar said sarcastically. "Excellent grouping with the painting. So serene. I feel at peace already."

"I like it. Where have you been? I haven't seen you in some time."

"Traveling. I wanted to see Machu Picchu, so I went."

"And was it wonderful? All that it is cracked up to be?"

Nikonar shrugged his shoulders. He could not care less.

"It was old, just like you. I had a feeling you wanted to see me, so here I am."

Bale laughed at his insolence then descended gracefully into a chair across from the huge, hulking Russian. The two vampires gazed at each other across the vast space. He loved the audacity of this room. The vast amounts of money and blood and fear and death it had taken to decorate it thrilled him every time he set foot in this opulent chamber. Even the air in here smelled expensive and decadent, laced with the thin, barely perceptible, coppery tang of blood that only a vampire could detect.

Such atmosphere!

The look they shared was almost, not quite but almost, tinged with love, not unlike a father and a son might look at each other. In a sense, Bale was his father, having made him what he was in that barn outside what would one day be Minsk in the year 1265.

Nikonar had willingly, gladly stepped into Bale's embrace to accept the dark gift. Of all the recipients Bale had known over the many centuries, Nikonar was the only one he felt was truly and completely born to this existence.

The weather had been freezing and healthy victims were tough for Bale to come by that winter. He had attempted to, with great disgust, suck blood from a woman who had just died from the cold. Bale sank his teeth into her scrawny neck but was stunned to find her blood frozen fast in her veins. Revolted, he spat the jelly-like goo out onto the snow.

Nikonar, traveling on the roads that evening, had come across Bale when they both sought shelter for the night. Keeping his true self a secret, Bale shared the space with him and a few cows and pigs, anxious to hear the huge Russian's story. Men of Nikonar's size were extremely rare in those days.

However, seeing that Nikonar appeared slightly weakened from hunger and travel, Bale easily slaughtered one of the pigs and served up the food to the Russian, marveling at how the repast quickly brought strength and vitality back to his large frame. Fed and comfortable, Nikonar told Bale the story of his life as a metalsmith, crafting exquisite but deadly weapons for the royalty and wealthy denizens of Europe. Bale found him fascinating, noting with relish that Nikonar loved and worshipped beauty and instruments of death.

The times had been difficult though for Nikonar, of which his tattered clothing and pale skin gave ample evidence. Bale spoke of wealth and power and absolute control and noted with some satisfaction how the Russian hung on every word, hungry for what riches he knew instinctively lay in Bale's world.

So, Bale took him, feeding himself and in turn feeding the Russian again, this time from his own veins. The conversion was quick, due in most part, Bale believed, because Nikonar truly wanted this life, or absence thereof. Although dead and no longer goal oriented to pursue a healthy human life filled with relationships and accomplishments, most vampires pursued the toys and wealth the world had to offer, and oh, was that to Nikonar's liking.

Immediately, upon his death, Nikonar vomited up what was left of the hog he had eaten. He tore the tattered clothing from his body and nakedly walked fearlessly in the freezing winter of Russia, plowing through ice and snowbanks to the nearest home. Upon entering, he slaughtered the entire family inside, then went through their clothing at his leisure until he was satisfied with his new raiment.

Bale watched the entire spectacle, perched like the all-knowing owl on a thick ice-covered tree branch outside the home. Nikonar emerged looking happy, fit and every inch the aristocrat he now knew in his non-beating heart that he was.

Bale marveled at his creation then, the same way he marveled looking at him lounging leisurely in front of the fireplace. Nikonar was his own master, killing and dominating the world around him, but sooner or later, wherever in the world he might be, Nikonar always returned to find Bale, his father, companion, mentor and ultimately his true master.

"There have been a lot of purchases on stock for Schwermut recently," Bale began. "Forty thousand shares just the other day. I've been tracking a huge influx of cash coming from Germany, but all the accounts are blind ones, no name attached. I didn't think much of it until the purchase came through for Schwermut. Delancey is brokering the transactions."

"Really? Why would anyone want to buy that shit? It's just one of your phony holding companies, isn't it?"

"Yes, exactly. Why would anyone want it? Something is... happening..."

"I think you're seeing ghosts where none exist. You just haven't had a good fight in a long time. You're bored."

"You think so?"

"Yes, and I have kept up with the news here, you know. All of those bodies left lying around...tsk, tsk Bale. Whatever are you doing? The police are running around with their panties bunched up to their ears."

"You think that is me? Since when would I be so sloppy?"

"Since when indeed! Ghosts, bodies, mysterious money

pouring in from Europe. Lies, spies and pigs might fly! It just makes me hungry. If you think someone is playing games with you, they'll show themselves soon enough. What do you have to worry about?"

"Nothing I suppose."

"Exactly. However, it will be great sport if someone is about to fuck with you. I want a front-row seat. I love coliseum events, and I'm so envious you got to see the real thing, by the way. In the meantime, I'm hungry. Come with me. I found a great little spot on the west side I think you'll love."

Nikonar drove his deep purple Ferrari to a small club called The Black Light. Inside was a sea of young, beautiful people smashed against each other, writhing to the pounding beat of the metal band playing behind overlapping sheets of Mylar to diffuse the heavy, deafening sound.

He waded right in, finding a beautiful young woman who was immediately drawn to his frighteningly compelling, exotic looks. No one could resist looking at a vampire, unless they wanted to move with obscurity. He watched as Bale pushed slowly into the crowd, which parted like a wave before him, until he reached Nikonar and the woman.

The young woman Nikonar had picked pushed herself up against him, dancing erotically, losing herself in the electric, amatory feel of his touch. Bale came up behind her, pushing her against Nikonar. In such close proximity to two vampires who focused all their attention on her, she was drunk with the sensations, reeling on her feet.

Bale sandwiched her between himself and Nikonar, and they matched rhythm, swaying hypnotically as they both ran their hands over her. Bale was becoming excited and reached his hands around her to grasp Nikonar's jacket, squeezing her tightly between them, using the Russian's expensively tailored lapels for leverage.

Slowly, Nikonar backed away from Bale and his prize, then he wandered into the thick wall of people dancing away with each other. As a courtesy, whenever he and Bale were hunting together, the first conquest belonged to his maker.

Bale wrapped his arms around her and moved slowly around the dance floor with her, letting her toes dangle. There was no rush, and there wasn't anything he liked better than to take a victim while surrounded by humans who were completely oblivious to what he was doing. He loathed humans and sought to extend their pain, suffering and agony as long as he could.

Her breath came in ragged gasps as she started to lose consciousness, giving way to the erotic sensations he was bringing to her. She could feel the dampness in her panties, and gave full permission to her body to feel the tingling sensations of an impending orgasm. She couldn't believe her good luck. Never had she been able to reach orgasm completely with a man, and always waited until the click of the door after he left to reach under her bed for her vibrator to bring herself to glorious climax but now, just dancing with this intense, dark man who held her so tightly, she could feel the climax rushing at her. She could barely believe her luck and to think, she was just going to stay at home tonight.

Bale ran his hands down the front of her body, cupping her breasts and tugging at the hair along the back of her neck with his teeth. She came, hard, convulsing against him just as Bale sunk his fangs into her neck. She hardly noticed; her body was jerking so violently. Nikonar wandered back to the two of them, leaned over and bit into the other side of her neck. Together in a matter of seconds, he and Bale had drained her body completely.

Nikonar easily picked up her lifeless body and carried it to the side of the room where he let it drop into a small red chair. He glanced quickly around the room. No one noticed what was happening at all.

"Leave her there," Bale said.

Nikonar looked into Bale's intense blue eyes, suspicious of what was going on. He shook his head.

"Yes," Bale went on, "leave her there."

What was he thinking? They never left their victims to be found. Was he actually playing some sort of game, leaving bodies all over Los Angeles? What the hell was he doing?

Bale smiled sweetly at him and walked away. Hesitant at first, Nikonar finally moved away from her and followed Bale outside. As soon as they were strolling through the evening breeze, Nikonar popped a toothpick into his mouth and worked it back and forth between his teeth. He would have to wait for Bale to explain his little game.

That is just the way things worked between them.

"So?" Bale asked calmly, "Machu Picchu? Did you have pleasant weather at least? I'm dying to hear more."

Chapter Six

Even as the limo carrying Amanda to her home in the hills slid slowly through the night, Villicus restlessly but happily made his way back through the palatial penthouse that was his new Los Angeles home. With ease, he tore into other containers stacked through the place and then his luggage, finding the perfect outfit to wear out seeing the city, taking in the sights and making his first kill on American soil.

Briefly, he had thought that Amanda might be the perfect first victim. After all, he knew Delancey had other competent brokers who could further his financial goals. But there was something about her, something that really caught his attention. Was it her humor, her beauty? He would need to study her further, to see if what caught his fancy about her might reveal itself later.

Satisfied with the Armani suit he wore - deep black with a silky white Cupro shirt opened part way down his chest - he raked his fingers through his long hair, redoing the clasp that held the gathered length down his back. Standing in his study, examining with relish the banks of monitors that gave him such an expansive eye of his new world, he shook his head gently, listening to the gentle clink chink of the silver chains looped at the back of his head.

He watched with satisfaction a website showing stock sales and market activity throughout the world. Leaning forward as the readout for Schwermut scrolled by, Villicus smiled broadly when he saw his new purchase had already affected the stock. The numbers were clicking higher even as he watched. His smile resembled more of a snarl, lips sliding back over teeth that briefly lengthened in front, then retreated again.

Absentmindedly, he clacked his teeth together.

He wrote an email to Amanda, asking her to sell all of the Schwermut stock then match purchases with another company called the Radikale Holding Company. After hitting the send key, he powered down the computer and headed out.

Snatching up the keys to the car he knew waited below the building in slot 19A, Villicus walked hastily to the private elevator that would carry him down. Having studied Amanda's use of the key to activate the system inside, he quickly figured out how to navigate his way to the basement.

The elevator gently and silently stopped and the sumptuous brushed-metal doors slid open. Dozens of incredibly expensive cars, all neatly parked in their own slots, covered the near acre of dull grey concrete and thick, paint-flaked pipes, some with rust dripping from them. The harsh lights from the fluorescent panels hanging from the ceiling gave everything the appearance of a moonscape—endless, dramatic, but devoid of life.

Villicus stepped out onto the concrete floor, enjoying the hollow ring his heels made on the hard surface. He could just hear a tiny skittering sound from across the parking area and knew it was made by rats, aware of his presence, rushing over each other to get away from him. Other than the vermin inhabiting this dreary space, Villicus knew he was alone, not another soul around. Listening to his footsteps, he noticed they sounded much like his own pacing in St. Bartholoma's cathedral not so long ago. He stopped for a moment and leaned his head back, dropping his jaw open, then yowled triumphantly into the silent space, letting his roar bounce off the walls. Chuckling now, most pleased with himself and his prowess, Villicus followed the numbers and letters along the wall until he located 19A.

There was his new car—a sleek, black Maserati Quattroporte Coupe—waiting for him like a finely sculpted metal and chrome serpent. Villicus wrinkled his nose at the dull concrete pillars and walls surrounding his elegant car and made a mental note to order the building superintendent to hang fabric, or some sort of tapestry, on the sickly grey cinder blocks. Paint was out of the question. Fabric and artistry were required to please him.

Unlocking the door, he opened the car then slid neatly inside, folding himself into the deep contoured seat. He tinkered with some of the knobs on the dash, then located the ignition. Turning the key, he gunned the engine to life and reveled at how the thunder of the car's power echoed in the dank, concrete space, much like his roar had earlier.

He was an engine.

While still in Europe, he had practiced driving a variety of cars. He would steal what he wanted, then force the owner to teach him how to drive it before he ripped their head off.

Villicus rested his finger ever so lightly along the top of the dash, feeling the tremor of power in their tips. Toying with the gas pedal, he revved the twin-turbocharged V8 engine, barely sensing any more vibration coming into the cabin because of the exquisite engineering but well aware of the power. It was all his.

Slamming the car into reverse, Villicus launched the vehicle out of slot 19A and spun it around, barely missing a Rolls Royce and cherry '74 Charger. He sped along, looking for the exit, finally noticing the enormous metal mesh doorway across the cavernous room, just as the concierge had described it. Gunning the engine, he sped towards it, trusting the gizmo hanging from his keys would indeed activate the door. He knew it must. After all, having paid millions for his new home, he, like most wealthy people, assumed everything would work as he demanded it must.

With satisfaction, he noticed the massive door shuddering as it began to heave itself up along thick metal chains attached to the sides. He had the car up to nearly 60 miles an hour by the time he reached the exit, barely giving the door enough time to clear the top of the car. Squeaking under with just inches to spare, he rocketed up onto the Avenue of the Stars, nearly killing several people walking serenely along the well-landscaped boulevard. They leapt out of his way, many landing in the nearby shrubbery and ornamental ponds.

The tires of the car cleared the pavement as he reached the zenith of the ramp and soared across one entire lane of the six-lane road before hitting the asphalt. He accelerated the moment rubber hit the road. With delight, Villicus easily navigated past the other cars, many swerving madly to avoid slamming into him or each other. His heightened senses allowed him to careen around objects at high speed with just centimeters to spare. He sailed between two cars, making his own lane between the startled drivers, and then ran a red light, disappearing into the heavy traffic jamming Santa Monica Blvd.

Without music or talk radio to keep him company, Villicus drove on through the night, leaning forward from time to time to peer out at the massive buildings and expensive homes running along both sides of the street. The only sounds were the deep thrumming from the powerful engine and his fingers tapping on the black steering wheel. He watched whole crowds of people, his new cattle, walking quickly along the sidewalks as if they really thought they had someplace to get to.

Slowing his ride, he turned onto Sunset Blvd and watched with fascination the circus of people, lights and crammed storefront windows packed with expensive merchandise. He made note of the stores still open this late at night and knew he would have some splendid shopping sprees to enjoy very soon.

"I wonder what's on sale?" Villicus asked himself, roaring with laughter at his own joke.

Near the ocean, he found a side street near a club that looked interesting. He pulled the car up to a harried looking parking lot attendant who frantically tried to wave him away. Villicus ignored him and stepped out of the car, leaving the engine running.

"I'll be back shortly," he told the angry man who rushed up to him.

"Look, buddy! Ain't no room left here. It's Friday night. No parking...," the man's frantic, loud outburst trailed off the closer he got to Villicus.

"What?" Villicus asked him amiably.

"No, ah, no, nothing man. I'll have your car right here when you get back."

"I'm sure of it," again Villicus said sweetly, as he strode around the befuddled man and headed towards the club.

Nearing the entrance, Villicus watched an idling limo hovering near the door. Several inebriated people, one woman supported on either side by two men several years her junior, headed towards the passenger door. At least fifty pounds overweight, gut hanging out over her tight pants, she was weaving badly.

"My little cuppy cakes, that's what you are. Cuppy cuppy cuppy cakes," She slurred heavily.

One of the men managed to slip out from under her ponderous arm and popped the limo's door open. Losing her support and falling to one side, her remaining companion shoved her weight forward, and she flopped neatly into the backseat. Villicus stood quietly in the shadows, laughing at the absurd show. God, he loved humans and their ridiculous attempts to have a good time. They really had no idea.

The two men wrestled her into an upright position and managed to get in on either side of her. As the car pulled away from the curb, just as the door began to close, Villicus could see them groping her with rough, rude hands, as she giggled insanely, singing out the cuppy cake song again. Belching a thin, foul veil of exhaust, the limo driver sped away from the curb with the overworked parking attendant frantically waving him away from Villicus car. Flying by, the driver flipped off the attendant then disappeared into the night.

Hearing a slight shuffle behind him, further into the shadows of the alley behind the club, Villicus spun around to see a man coming slowly up behind him. Studying him carefully, quickly seeing every detail about him in the dark with his vampire eyes, Villicus saw the man pause as he approached, one hand held out. He appeared to be some sort of street beggar, a common sight in any century.

"Hey buddy, ya got a buck?" the disheveled man asked Villicus.

"I don't have a buck," Villicus said quietly, speaking each word slowly and evenly.

The man, appearing a bit angry, got closer to Villicus.

"What the fuck, buddy? I saw the ride you just got out of and…hey, well…," his words trailed off as he neared the vampire.

The man froze in place, his hand still out, his eyes locked onto Villicus as he started to tremble.

Villicus studied the odd bit of flotsam standing before him as a startled and fearful expression spread over the panhandler's face. Instinctively aware that something terrifying was standing in front of him, like a mouse cornered by a bored cat, the man's cheeks went slack, and his mouth fell open. Loving the reaction, Villicus reached into his pocket and removed a thick roll of cash. He peeled off a hundred-dollar bill, wadded it up then, neatly tapped it into the man's open mouth.

The shaken panhandler spat the money out, then turned and ran. The money lay on the ground, slowly opening up until a small gust of wind caught it and blew it further down the sidewalk.

Inside the club, fairly vibrating off its foundation with the pounding music and pulsating bodies engaging in legal foreplay, Villicus waded into the humans, loving how they crashed into him, bouncing hard off of his impenetrable body. A few threw him startled looks as they watched him move unscathed through the room towards an upholstered counter bar at the back. Festooned with nets and huge neon sculptures of seahorses, fish and shells, a life size King Neptune lorded above the bar, brandishing a colossal trident whose tips pulsated off and on with blue and white lights.

Villicus found an empty bar stool and perched on top, half turning to watch the crowd of beautiful people mashing about the room like an enormous, overcrowded ant farm. He chose obscurity now, blending into the background as he studied his potential victims. Oh, to pick the right one.

"Get something for ya?" the bartender shouted at him.

A lovely brunette woman, seeming to oil out of the crowd, slid seductively onto the stool next to Villicus.

"I'll have a greyhound," she told the bartender, favoring him with a sly wink.

"And for you?" the bartender asked Villicus again.

"Nothing for me right now."

The bartender moved away to ready her drink.

"A greyhound?" Villicus asked, confused by her order.

"It's a drink, silly."

"Is it?"

Villicus quickly ran his eyes over her body, noting her expensive clothing, fake jewelry and the way she pointed her shapely knees at him, thighs slightly parted. She appeared to be as much on the prowl as he was.

"Yes. Vodka and grapefruit juice. You've never had one?"

He shook his head no as the bartender quickly returned with her drink. Villicus peeled a hundred-dollar bill from the wad of cash he had been carrying with him and handed it to the bartender, then waved him away, but not before the brunette greedily noticed this transaction. A sweet smile spread over Villicus's ripe lips. He had found her, his meal for the night, and she had come right to him.

"You're not having anything?" she asked sweetly.

"Not yet."

"Oh. What do you like to drink?"

Leaning forward, studying her closely, Villicus admired how perfectly her makeup was applied. It must have taken her hours to prepare for her night out. He slid his finger over her cheek. She shuddered under his touch, and he noticed her eyes glaze over slightly. She was his. He knew it. Now, to make some sport of this, to enjoy each moment of life she had left, before he wrenched it from her.

So engrossed with her, Villicus was unaware of a pair of eyes trained on him from across the room. Seated at the largest booth in the place, Howley Bennett, surrounded by his entourage of toadies, watched with fascination the seduction taking place at the bar. The sea of idiots between them undulated to the music, rubbing up against and groping each other, but Howley was oblivious to them.

One of those in his group asked him if he wanted anything, but Howley shook his head with some force. Startled by his abrupt response, the man crouched back into the deep padded seats of the booth, rapidly turning his attention back to the other drunken fools at the table.

Howley dropped several large bills in front of the man, then started to move fast, too quickly for the people at his table. Four people, jammed into the seat next to him, spilled out onto the floor like clowns exiting a tiny car, making room for him to exit.

He watched quietly as Villicus and the young woman exited the bar, the mass of people parting like the Red Sea as the elegant vampire and his date for the night crossed to the door. Waiting for a few moments, so as not to be noticed, Howley quickly but quietly followed the pair into the night.

Villicus led her outside where she started to stumble, falling more and more under his influence. He put one arm around her, supporting her like the two men had shored up the drunken woman into the limo earlier. No one paid them any attention as he led her into a tiny park at the ocean's edge.

Once in the park, she fell, so Villicus easily picked her up with one arm, dangling her effortlessly over his hip as he headed to the base of a statue and dropped her onto the ground with a thud. Her head snapped back, banging hard into the solid base of the

sculpture, a large alabaster-white reproduction of the Archangel Ariel, who graced this small esplanade.

"Who are you?" she slurred at him.

"I'm your best friend."

Villicus kneeled before her as he ran his fingers lightly over the delicate skin of her neck. Loving this feeling of transition into his full, true self, Villicus ran his hands greedily over every inch of her body, feeling her breasts, her thighs. He felt his eyes turning completely black, taking on a dull inky hue. She saw what was happening but was unable to do anything except lay there and let him take her–willingly.

Fascinated, she watched him flex his jaw open, his teeth lengthening to sharp points. Reaching up, she grasped the ends of the stone angel's wings and held on. Instinctively, she braced herself.

"Tell me what you're feeling," Villicus hissed at her, his hands continuing to explore her body as she moaned from the sensations he was teasing from her body.

With a swiftness that amazed even him, the woman lunged

forward and kissed him hard, puncturing her lips on Villicus's exposed fangs. Her blood trickled into his mouth, sending him completely over the edge. Slamming her down, he kissed her back equally as hard, but for other reasons. He was not succumbing to a sexual urge. He was slipping into the madness unique to the vampire that drives them to kill.

Roughly, he pulled his mouth away, studying her face as her body writhed under his touch. A small trickle of her blood ran from his lips, which he licked away.

"Tell me what it feels like. Tell me!" he demanded.

Weakly, she shook her head, and her body started to convulse from the orgasm he was giving her.

Furious that she could not or would not answer, Villicus grabbed her thick mane of hair, yanked her head back, then, ripped into her throat like a rattlesnake striking a target. He had pulled her half upright in the process, and as her life ebbed away and his thirst and rage began to slake, he settled slowly back to his knees, letting her slide down with him. His sense of the world came rushing back at him.

Suddenly aware of being watched, and watched closely, Villicus spun about, his eyes still black pools of death. Hovering next to him, mere inches away, Howley stared into those savage pools.

"Was that good for you?" Howley asked quietly, a slight trace of humor in his voice.

Villicus let go of the woman's body, which slumped over onto the ground. A few drops of blood fell from his mouth as his features reverted back into his human guise.

"Watch the shoes, would ya? They're Bruno Maglis," Howley admonished him, moving his toes out of the way of the falling blood.

Slipping a linen handkerchief from his pocket, Villicus wiped his lips then stepped towards this interloper who had watched him so quietly. Suddenly, his eyes widened in surprise.

"Howley?" Villicus asked, completely shocked and amazed.

"Where the hell have you been?" Howley asked nonchalantly but clearly as shocked as Villicus.

Both rose and then embraced each other as the dead woman

lay in a crumpled heap between their feet. Quickly, Howley and Villicus grasped her wrists and then tossed her lifeless body into a deep canal draining out into the ocean. As they turned to walk away from her, before the splash had even subsided, Villicus tossed his soiled handkerchief into the water after her. It opened like a flower in the salty water, then sank a short distance below the surface and came to rest on a submerged rock.

Chapter Seven

The moon sailed further along the night sky, casting long and mysterious reflections onto the ocean. While crabs and small sharks dined on the remains of the woman tossed into the dark canal, entire banks of lights snapped on at the Bad Wolf film production offices in Hollywood across town.

Howley banged through a pair of French doors, kicking them open with gusto. This was something he apparently liked to do, as evidenced by the scars on the walls. He sailed into the room like a returning conqueror, passing enormous movie posters plastered on the walls shouting out B movie titles like Basher, Mayhem's King and The Shoppers of Death—all action, violent action, with tons of T&A.

The far wall held an enormous version of the Bad Wolf logo. It was a black, lupine graphic outlined completely in red neon, casting crimson colored light onto the expensive, albeit gaudy furnishings. As Howley moved through the room, sensors picked up his presence, and loud rock music kicked on, followed by more banks of lights.

A massive TV screen fluttered to life, and it was tuned to multiple channels—weather, news, sports, movies, TV shows and a few screens devoted to interviews and stories about Hollywood. Thankfully, because so many channels were running at the same time, the audio had been muted.

A popcorn machine rattled to life along with a couple of pinball machines and other assorted games including VR masks and huge video game computers and their monitors. It was a massive playpen for even the most hardcore gamer geek.

Howley was home.

Villicus came in behind him, taking in all the gaudiness, particularly the overriding use of red in the color schemes. A small smile tugged at his lips as he remembered that particular detail about his friend. Villicus sucked at his teeth, still tasting the woman who had died in his arms less than an hour before.

Howley moved around to the other side of his gigantic teak desk covered with phones and executive toys that operated the lights and music. Just as he flopped into his red leather chair, he hit one button that dropped the volume of the pounding music down.

"When did you get here?" Howley asked him.

"Just earlier tonight. You?"

"Oh, not long ago really. Forty, forty-five years maybe. I've lost count. I was in Italy but got tired of all that fucking art."

"And you came here? This is such a visible lifestyle. Aren't you concerned people will notice that you haven't aged?"

"Hell no. It's Hollywood. No one ages here. It's a great herd, beautiful, dumb and plentiful. They get off the buses every day from every damn place in this country you can think of, looking for, well, all of this!"

Howley gestured about the room at the movie memorabilia that dripped from the walls and shelves. He stabbed at another button on his desk, killing the music completely, then studied Villicus in earnest.

"So, what happened to you? I thought you were dead, as in, really dead and gone from the planet. We all did."

"The royal *we*?" Villicus joked.

"What?" he hollered, not getting the joke. "Jesus, the last time I saw you, that fucking Black Death was parading around the countryside, and those damn Holy Wars kept going on and on and on and on! All that damn tramping back and forth. The Inquisition was kinda fun though."

"Sorry I missed all that."

"Yeah well, what do you mean missed it? Where did you go? Fucking Tibet?"

"Do you remember Nikonar?"

Howley clammed up and leaned back into the deep pit of his chair, letting a soft sigh escape through his teeth.

Absentmindedly, he chewed on one finger as he studied the stony-faced vampire seated across from him.

"Yeah. He's here, you know," Howley answered solemnly.

"I know. And Bale?" Villicus asked quickly.

Frustrated, Howley rubbed his face with his hands and tried unsuccessfully to read the unfathomable poker face Villicus was showing him.

"Yeah, him too," Howley muttered, "but I'm guessing you knew that already. Question for the ages though, my friend, does Bale know that you're here?"

Chapter Eight

Amanda arrived at work just as the sun rose. Riding up in the posh elevator, she rolled her eyes as the sappy Muzak drenching the upholstered space. She braced for the stop, squelched a yawn, and shook herself all the way awake as the doors opened for another day at Delancey. The noise from the day traders, booming down the hallways, indicated it was going to be a busy day. They had a lot of catching up to do after the drama with the hacker the day before.

Nodding pleasantly to the receptionist Jilly, she made her way across the stone floors, wincing at the clack her tiny heels made. She rode up on her toes, trying to be quiet. A childish habit, she knew, but her way of not drawing attention to herself.

Amanda was extremely focused on her work and her future, and although she was thrilled when her achievements garnered accolades, she herself loathed any moments in the limelight. She could never be just Amanda.

"Let your work speak for you," her mother had admonished her again and again. Apparently, the words sunk in.

Grateful when she reached the carpeted hallway so she could walk normally again, Amanda hiked down the hall to her office, enjoying the morning routines of the secretaries moving quietly around their cubicles that fronted the offices. She was aware of the subtly changing landscapes for these people–the new drawings their children did for them, photos of weddings and new babies–all evidence of a life Amanda had never known and doubted she ever would. Tilting her head down, pretending she was reading a memo, she hustled past these people who actually seemed to have lives.

The systems better be up and fully functional, Amanda hoped to herself. She needed to bury herself back in her work.

"No hackers today," she whispered out loud, secretly threatening the unknown interloper who had dared enter their bastion through the executive men's washroom.

Rounding a corner, past a gorgeous framed Jasper Johns print, she caught sight of herself in the polished glass and stopped to admire the pendant that Villicus had given her the night before. She fingered the gem hanging delicately from her neck, loving the delicious, perfect feel of its cut surface, then chided herself for having kissed him.

What was she thinking?

Here was a man who could have anything or anyone in the world. What would he want with her? Shaking her head again and trying to wipe away the slight blush riding up in her cheeks, she noticed Paul Peter up ahead, moving anxiously about his cubicle.

"Paul, what is it?" Amanda asked, as she paused by the door to her office.

"Nothing!" he chirped up, a bit too rapidly, as he made a great show of rearranging everything on his already pristine desk.

Amanda sensed something was up but also knew this man quite well. He had worked for her since she had arrived at Delancey and was the closest thing she had to family. Smiling to herself and knowing he was bursting with some secret to tell her, she pushed her office door open and headed inside. Purposely, she left the door open as an invitation for Paul Peter to join her.

Before she could even settle in behind the desk, Paul Peter bustled in with her coffee and morning mail. Out of the corner of her eye, she watched him cross the room. Turning on her computer, she keyed open the email, her usual morning ritual, and found the message from Villicus asking her to match purchases with the Radikale Holding Company.

Amanda's brow furled as she did a quick bit of research. It was a publicly held company, so there was trading going on with stocks, and then she found that it was the sister company to Schwermut.

Something seemed very odd here; however, whatever her client wants her client gets. She double checked how much stock Villicus currently owned from Schwermut then submitted a purchase order for the same amount of Radikale, completing the transaction with the sale of the Schwermut stocks.

She hoped like hell that Villicus knew what he was doing. What she was doing just bordered, slightly, on unethical behavior because these large purchases then rapid sales could damage the companies and could be viewed by the trade commission as an attack. As soon as she finished executing the orders, Paul Peter was right there, in front of her desk with a huge silly grin on his face.

He set her coffee down then fumbled with the mail. A neat-looking envelope slipped out of his grasp and hit the floor next to her desk.

"What's that?" she asked as she leaned forward quickly, trying to see it.

Paul Peter was too quick for her and had retrieved it before she could really see it, covering it up with both of his hands.

"What!" he cried out, then started waving the envelope quickly in the air. "This thing? What, this? This envelope I have in my hands here?"

Whatever the big secret was hidden in that envelope, it had fired Paul Peter up. She had seen him enjoying himself before, often at her expense, however something was just way over the top, so she settled down to play the game with him. She had known him too long and was well aware that he was only going to reveal the surprise when it suited him.

Amanda snatched up her coffee and sipped it with great pleasure.

"Give it to me right now, or I may have to hurt you."

He continued to shield the envelope until he could move it directly in front of her, and then slid his fingers apart, revealing an elaborate, gold, embossed seal on the back. Seeing her eyes widen in surprise, he slowly turned it around so she could see her name on the front, hand-written by a talented calligrapher.

Impatiently, she snatched it from his hand and then motioned Paul Peter into a chair across from her desk.

"You, rotten little toadie," she chided him. "How could you hide this from me!"

Paul Peter curled his fingers in front of his broadly smiling mouth and motioned for her to hurry up as she slowly pulled a letter opener from her desk.

As if disarming a letter bomb, Amanda carefully separated the gold seal on the back from the paper and then gently slid the card out that was inside. Just as carefully, after she had set the opener down and moved her coffee well away in case it spilled, she turned the card over.

"It's what I think it is, isn't it!" Paul Peter cried out to her.

Amanda read the card slowly, not answering him or even looking at him.

"Oh, come on!" he cried out again. "You gotta show me!"

Amanda smiled like a happy cat and turned the card around for him to see. Paul Peter leapt out his chair and jumped up and down a few times.

"I knew it! I knew it! I knew it!"

"Is this real?" she asked him.

"What...wha...oh Amanda, I would never prank something like that!"

He leaned forward to read it more closely.

The front of the expensive white card stated simply "Checkers".

Using his pinky finger, he lifted the card and read the invitation inside out loud.

"You are cordially invited."

Amanda handed him the card, and Paul Peter sat back down, reading it again to himself. She just shook her head in amazement.

"This can't be right."

"Oh, Amanda," he scolded her gently. "You, more than anyone here, deserve this. Don't be so surprised. All the money your accounts have been generating, especially Herr Shanks... you have definitely earned this."

Amanda started first, giggling softly and tapping out a soft rhythm on her desktop. Paul Peter kept time with her, tapping his feet on the floor. Their shared celebration was cut short by a harsh rapping at her door.

They both stopped and looked to see Mark leaning in, smiling and giving Amanda a weak wave. He stared Paul Peter down, who quickly placed the Checkers invitation on her desk before scurrying out to the safety of his cubicle.

Mark pointed to the card on her desk.

"Got mine this morning too. Quite an honor. This is your first time to be invited, isn't it?"

Amanda nodded curtly.

"You going? I mean, it would be bad form not to go."

"I suppose you're right. How many from Delancey have been invited?"

"Well, Richmond, of course."

"Of course."

"You, me, Ralston was invited I believe, along with Chase and Dorchester. A few others. So, you going?"

She again nodded curtly.

"Go with me then. Be my date. It would look good...partners from the same group. Like a power front. I've been there before and can show you the ropes."

Amanda leaned back and watched him warily.

"Oh, thanks Mark, but...I think I'll be asking someone else to go with me."

"Oh? You seeing someone?"

She nodded.

Doing a very poor job of hiding his disgust with her, Mark turned to leave, calling out over his shoulder, "Oh well, fine...I guess I'll see you there then."

"Yes. I'm looking forward to it," she whispered sarcastically to thin air.

Mark's departure left an icy chill in her office, which was quickly warmed up when Paul Peter bounced back in.

"You will be asking someone to go with you?" he asked brightly.

"You were listening at the door again."

He gave her his best "NO – not me!" look. She actually laughed at his antics this time.

Amanda checked the digital clock on her computer. It read 6:30 a.m., much too early to call.

Without looking up, she pointed a finger towards her door and hollered at Paul Peter, "Get out! Close the fucking door! Stop spying on me! Bring me the morning tally sheets. NOW!"

Smiling ear to ear, he ducked out, muttering to her he was going online immediately to start scoping out dresses.

Amanda had already tuned him out and was carefully wording an email to Villicus.

Chapter Nine

The sunrise at the shore was quite pretty that morning. A cluster of palm trees cast lovely, dappled shadows across the small group of police officers and detectives watching divers fish for the body of the date that Villicus and Howley had tossed into the canal the night before.

Detective Kim Barnstall turned to look out over the waves and noticed a group of surfers straddling their colorful boards, watching them. On the other side of the canal, her partner James was searching the area with some uniforms, looking for any evidence that might shed some light on what had happened to this once lovely woman, now being manhandled up onto the bank by the divers and two men from the coroner's office.

The men on shore slid her body into an opened body bag. It was clear, by her incredibly pale color that most, if not all of her blood, had been removed.

Kim's attention was drawn to the actions of one of the men, who straddled the body almost lasciviously, studying the dead woman intently. Just as she was about to approach him to ask what it was he thought he was doing, she saw his hand whip down and fish a few crabs out of the body bag.

Kim stopped in her tracks and left him to his business.

The man who had fished the crabs out of the bag quickly zipped it closed. He and the other assistant from the coroner's office hefted it up and carried the body off to their waiting van.

"Detective Barnstall?"

Kim looked across the canal again, shielding her eyes from a few intense rays of light that fought their way through the canopy of palm fronds. She saw James standing further down the canal towards the ocean, motioning for her to come over. As she turned towards the footbridge, she saw the two divers crouching down in the canal with the water cutting across their face masks. They looked like enormous scary frogs that could see everything going on in both worlds—the air and the water. The image was more than a bit disturbing to Kim, even for a crime scene, so she picked up her pace.

Crossing to the other side, she moved over by James, who was staring intently into the water. The uniformed officers who had been searching the area with him were now stringing more yellow crime tape around the end of the canal, and the two divers, still squatting in the water, were slowly duck-walking forward. Montgomery was waving them towards a low grouping of rocks with his hands, then abruptly motioned for them to stop.

Kim moved up beside him and watched as the divers collected a discolored linen handkerchief.

Extremely pleased, she gently tapped him on the elbow, discreetly nodded her approval then walked away with a blushing James following.

"How are you doing Detective?" she asked him.

"Good. We are almost done here."

"Any idea who our victim was?"

Montgomery pointed to a woman's purse, already bagged and set on a pile of other items to be loaded up by forensics and taken downtown for the arduous work of sorting out what happened here.

"That was with her?"

"No. The bartender found it sitting on the bar and brought it to us. We compared the photo IDs in there with her face, what's left of it, and I'm pretty sure her name is Sondra Callahan."

"Sondra. Okay, good work. Pretty name. Any calls about her? Any missing person reports?"

"Yes, her roommates contacted the police about an hour ago, sure that something had happened to her."

"That's surprising. Usually it takes longer for roommates to report a missing person."

"Right. Ms. Callahan, though, had borrowed a car from one

of them to drive here last night, and that roommate needed it to get to work this morning."

"Ah. Did you locate the car?"

"Yes. Forensics is going over it now, then it will be towed downtown."

Kim believed the scene was pretty much done and she could leave the final bit of work to James, but he stopped her before she could get too far away.

She looked at him, concerned that he did not have the confidence yet to finish up the collection of items and evaluation of this gruesome crime scene. The moment she made eye contact with him though, it was clear that was not the case.

He motioned for her to follow him.

Together, they walked up to the statue where a forensic team was gathered. With great interest, Kim observed the pattern of blood drops that speckled the walkway and base of the statue.

"Wow. This is a first. Actual traces of blood at the scene. I would assume that our victim met her demise here."

"Most likely, and, since it does seem to be another of our horrible murders, this could be the break we had been hoping for."

Kim was doubly impressed with James and took a few photos of the blood with her cell phone to study when she got back to her desk.

The two of them walked around the statue of the Archangel Ariel, being careful to not disturb the forensic technicians.

"Well, I had high hopes for a moment there, but apparently this death still has a boatload of mysteries attached to it," Kim said.

"I checked and double checked, but other than the few drops on the sidewalk and the base of the statue, there isn't any other blood here, not that we have found yet, but we will look more."

"Okay, good. Let me know what you come up with."

He nodded and gave her a quick salute.

"Will do boss. You know it!"

"I want to be there with the coroner when they bring Sondra in," she said.

Kim started to back away.

"Absolutely! I'll finish up here and meet you downtown when we are done." James called after her.

She headed for her car and wondered, as she hurried along, if maybe, just maybe, they finally caught a break. James and his crew there had found something at the scene that they had not discovered before, and that was exciting. Where, though, were all the pints of bloods that Sondra was missing?

Chapter Ten

As pretty as the dawn could be in Los Angeles, the City of Angels really shone at night after the sun went down. Strategic views from the hills afforded gorgeous views of the jewel-like expanse.

Amanda stood on the balcony of her home, a neat two-bedroom stucco nestled into the side of the Hollywood Hills. She adored this house and bought it because of the tall trees on either side, blocking the view of her neighbors but beautifully framing the city laid out below. It was as if the city was hers and hers alone.

Somewhere down on Sunset Blvd., a movie premiere of some kind was going on. Huge klieg lights crisscrossed back and forth, gracefully fading out in the cloudless sky, lending an old Hollywood atmosphere to what she was sure was going to be an amazing night.

The sliding glass doors to her living room were open, and she could hear a discreet tapping from her front door just down the hallway. Biting her lips from nerves, she set down the elegant wineglass she had been holding and turned to step through the open glass doors. Catching sight of her reflection, Amanda smoothed down the gown she was wearing. She had to admit, Paul Peter had great taste. The floor length black Georgette gown with the short, white jacket was perfect—black and white, just like the Checkers' logo. The upturned collar of the jacket perfectly framed the necklace Villicus had given her.

Hurrying just a bit, she headed for the front door.

"Coming!" she called out.

Amanda did not even check the peephole in the door to see

who was there. She was certain who it would be.

Tugging the door open, she found Villicus waiting for her, dazzlingly attired in a tuxedo. She could feel the breath catching in her throat and a brief rush of insecurity. How was this man, this amazing looking creature, hers for the evening?

"Villicus! So good to see you. Come in," she said brightly.

He stepped across the threshold as Amanda took a few steps back to make room.

"You look incredible," she went on, trying not to stammer. "Every inch the lady killer."

Villicus stopped dead in his tracks and stared at her, his head cocking ever so slightly to one side. The confused look on his face shattered the last bit of self-control she had, and Amanda burst out laughing.

Covering her mouth, she looked away, trying to regain some composure, but it did not work. The moment she looked back into that confused face, she lost it completely, and her laughing turned into a loud, braying. Amanda could feel snot rising in her nose.

She retreated to the kitchen, cursing under her breath.

Villicus followed from a discreet distance and poked his head around the corner to see her dabbing her eyes with a paper towel. In her haste, she had pulled the roll too quickly, and a small pool of the paper was gathered around her feet.

He started to cross into the room to her, but she held her hand out, indicating he should wait.

"Please, just give me a second," she said, stifling the laughing fit that had grabbed her.

Standing perfectly still, his hands crossed behind his back, Villicus asked quietly, "Lady killer?"

Amanda stooped over and gathered up the excess paper towels, which she stuffed quickly into the garbage.

"It's a compliment."

"Is it?"

"Yes, but, ah, we should go. Checkers awaits!"

As they wound their way down through the hills, snug in Villicus's Maserati, Amanda was in heaven. He handled the car like it was an extension of himself, sensing where to turn even before the road curved one way or the other.

It was almost as if he could see in the dark, Amanda thought to herself.

"Thank you for inviting me," he said.

"Oh, thank you for coming. I just thought this could be a really good thing for you. Everyone who is anyone in the world of finance will be there tonight."

"Will they?"

"Since you were out of the loop, as you said, this could give you an opportunity to catch up."

"Those stocks I emailed you about…"

"I…did it! That caused quite a buzz."

"Did it?"

"The sale of Schwermut stock cracked their foundation… somewhat, especially after your purchase order for the Radikale stock. The Schwermut went for a drastically lower price than what you bought them for. I know this is none of my business, but did you plan on that?"

"Yes."

"You might be playing a dangerous game, Villicus."

He ignored the comment as Amanda wondered if maybe she was playing a dangerous game as well. What was she getting into with this man? What sort of scheme was he involved in?

Silently, they rode the last few miles to the Los Angeles Aquarium where the social event of the season was going on. Checkers was a milestone invitation for anyone who made their money by making money for other people. Brokers, traders, investors and bankers all desired to be on the list of invitees. They gathered once a year in their finest and took part in a silent auction which benefited a different charity each year. This year, according to the invitation, funds collected would be going to help aid in the relief of people hit by storms in the Pacific. A worthy cause, Amanda had thought and wondered if anyone attending tonight really cared.

Of course, they did not. Getting invited and being seen with those that liked being seen was all that mattered. And she wanted to be seen that night, especially on the arm of her wealthiest client. She could not wait to show him off and was already planning strategies on keeping the hooks of the other invitees out of him. This was all grossly unfair to Villicus she knew, but was secretly planning on making it up to him later that evening. Paul Peter had thought to also order her the most exquisite undergarments to go with the amazing gown she now wore. The evening was going to be perfect.

They rolled into the valet area of the parking lot, where over a dozen men scurried about helping people from their cars—Bentleys, Rolls Royce, Porsche, Mercedes Benz and more expensive rides. The valets were all attired in crisp black and white suits and, with well-trained moves, assisted those arriving for the event. As Villicus Maserati slowed to a stop, three of them descended upon his car. One helped him out, traded him a ticket for his keys then slid effortlessly into the front seat, immediately aware of where everything was on this car. The other two assisted Amanda, helping her up and out of the low car onto her high heels, all while keeping her gown from getting wrinkled or exposing too much ankle. She was loving every moment of it. These valets made everyone feel like royalty.

Villicus stood to one side, watching the valet drive off with his ride, so Amanda took the opportunity to start greasing the wheels for the evening. The sidewalk had numerous high-powered lights set into the ground, shining up at the Los Angeles Aquarium sign and some of the gorgeous foliage around the parking lot. She positioned herself in front of one of the lights, knowing her legs would be silhouetted perfectly through her gown. A light breeze rustled the hem of her garment, tickling her ankles. Perfect.

Villicus turned in her direction but seemed to be scanning the other vehicles in the area and barely saw her. Slightly embarrassed, especially when she noticed all the valets in the area staring at her, she quickly moved away from the light and took the arm Villicus offered to her. He continued to scan the cars in the lot, watching them carefully as they pulled in.

Perhaps he really was there just to be seen with all the moneymakers, she thought to herself. She was going to have to be a bit more patient and remain nimble with her strategy.

They made their way along the winding sidewalk, past blooming hyacinth and massive, heavy boughs of red and pink bougainvillea draped elegantly over trellises covering the main courtyard in front of the aquarium. The building itself was an impressive structure made up of massive walls of raw concrete embedded here and there with cast relief sculptures of the flora and fauna of the sea. A few of these concrete panels were separated by slivers of thick, Plexiglas sections of the inside display tanks, lit from inside so anyone in the main courtyard could look up and glimpse sharks, rays and a plethora of multicolored fishes gliding past these narrow windows. Amanda did not really have a clue as to the kinds of exhibits there might be inside but did remember reading that the building had cost $63.7 million dollars to build with an annual maintenance budget of $3.3 million dollars. That could buy a hell of a lot of fish!

With her fingers curled delicately around Villicus arm, they descended a few steps into the main courtyard and walked together towards the reception area where a slight bottleneck of people was forming. It was rare for interlopers to gain access to the coveted event, but it did happen sometimes, mostly by members of the press or junior brokers hoping to score some new clients. A series of tables flanked the entrance in a restrictive pattern, with just a narrow space between the last two before entering the building. About twenty people were gathered in front of the various tables, having their invitations checked against the master list.

Amanda began to slow down a bit as they approached the gathered group, but Villicus never paused, tugging her gently along with him. As if a gust of wind had parted a row of wheat, the people gathered in front of the tables stepped aside as he approached, staring intently at him. Amanda felt as if she were invisible and noticed more than one person with their mouth hanging open when they turned to see him. They could not take their eyes off of him.

One woman stepped forward and reached out tentatively with jewelry encrusted fingers to touch Villicus's but he grasped her fingertips lightly in his hand and gave it a gentle shake, then released her. Amanda was becoming a bit overwhelmed at the reaction these people had to him, but he must have sensed this because he tugged her own fingertips up higher on his arm and kept moving her forward.

"Good evening, Ms. Brax. Delightful to see you."

Paul Peter was standing behind one of the greeting tables, and his cheerful and loud greeting snapped Amanda out of the surreal cloud that was enveloping her.

"Paul!"

"Yes, ma'am, and may I say, you look...amazing," Paul said, as he winked at her.

"You should know," Amanda said, with equal, although secretive, gusto.

Paul looked over at Villicus and like many of the other people in the area, was stunned to silence. Blushing wildly, he awkwardly began stammering while straightening his already impeccable suit and fluttering his hands over his hair, looking for any unruly strands in his neat brush-cut do.

Trying to put him at ease, Amanda spoke again, "I didn't know you were going to be here tonight. What a nice surprise!"

"Oh, tonight, yes, I'm here tonight," Paul blurted, trying hard to recover his composure. "I signed up to assist. My way of getting to be here, you know..."

"Paul, this is Villicus Shanks," Amanda cut him off.

Villicus extended his hand, and Paul reached to take it, barely grasping his fingertips.

Gaining more composure, Paul said to him, "Wie geht es Ihnen?"

Villicus smiled politely, nodding his head in gratitude at hearing his native tongue.

"I'm very well, thank you," Villicus answered him back. "You know German."

"Some. Just a smidgen, really. My grandmother was from Berlin."

Amanda had stepped back a bit so the two could meet and shot Paul a dirty *oh now you tell me* look. Paul winked wickedly at her.

Giving Villicus a gentle shove, Amanda moved him past the tables.

"Come along, Mr. Shanks," she said playfully. "Oodles of fish await us."

"Oodles," Villicus parroted her word, clearly confused at the meaning.

"Come on, easier if I show you," Amanda chuckled at him, tugging him along.

"Enjoy the party!" Paul called out to them as they made their way past.

Just before they passed through the enormous open glass doors inside, Villicus stopped short and turned to look back out at the parking lot, watching more expensive rides slip quietly up to the smartly turned-out valets. Amanda watched him with curiosity.

"Did you forget something?"

Villicus seemed not to have heard her. He appeared to be miles away, watching with detached interest the events on the lot. Amanda felt truly invisible again.

Finally, he turned to her with the warmest smile she had seen from him and said, "No. I forgot nothing. Come, I'm dying to see this party. Let's go."

Chapter Eleven

Two valets in the lot cautiously motioned an enormous silver Mercedes forward as if they were guiding a 747 through a mismanaged barbed wire factory and did not want to scratch the paint. The car glided to a stop, its tinted windows obscuring the passengers inside.

One of the valets leaped around to the driver's side and reached out to open the door but took a step back as whoever was inside opened it instead. The young man, his cute little black bowtie slightly askew, forgot to breathe for a moment as he watched the dark-haired man step gracefully out onto a tarmac covered with a smattering of dried, stuck gum and dead bugs. The valet, his hand held part way out in front of him to accept the keys, froze in place.

Bale, oblivious to the frozen young man standing in front of him, turned to look towards the aquarium. Quickly, he rubbed his hands together, clearly savoring the party atmosphere, then tilted his head slightly to look down at the valet. Like a gunslinger flipping a gun around his finger, Bale spun his keys around on their ring several times and then released the bunch, sending them flying up into the air. The young valet, still in shock, finally burst into action and dove for them, catching the heavy cluster of keys before they hit the hood of the Mercedes.

Smiling sweetly at him, Bale reached out and straightened the young man's bow tie, then slapped him, just a bit too hard on the face, sending him back a few steps.

"Just a super, super job, my boy," Bale said quietly to him, enunciating each word with relish. "Really, a most excellent catch. You won't scratch my car now, will you?"

The young man shook his head dumbly.

The passenger door opened and Nikonar stepped out and up onto the sidewalk, towering over the other tiny valet, who looked like a garden ornament standing next to him. Nikonar smoothed out the jacket of his elaborate, black-velvet tuxedo and shook his golden hair loose, so it sat just so on his shoulders. Bale laughed while he watched him primping.

The valet next to him, his mouth hanging open, slowly handed a ticket stub up to the Russian, who made a great show of bending down low to retrieve it from him. His alabaster face stopped just centimeters away, staring intently at the small piece of paper.

"And so, what is this?" Nikonar toyed with him, rolling his dark eyes up to look at him.

"Your ticket, your parking ticket, ah, sir. So, you know, we can give you your car back when you, ah, finish, at the party," the young man stammered as he gestured lamely over his shoulder.

"I suppose we should keep that, then," Nikonar said facetiously as he reached forward slowly, caressing the valet's fingers with his own as he slid the ticket from his hand. The young man hyperventilated and backed quickly away, nearly falling onto the lawn.

Bale had come around to join him on the sidewalk, and the two vampires strolled towards the aquarium together.

"The herd is very, very pretty tonight," Nikonar exclaimed. "I approve."

"It is indeed," Bale responded cheerfully with just a trace of guile in his silky voice. "I do so enjoy when they dress for the occasion. Don't they just look primped, plump and primed?"

Bale and Nikonar casually approached the greeting tables, oblivious to the crowd of people parting for them as others had done for Villicus a few minutes earlier. Bale hesitated, just a fraction of a second. For just a heartbeat, his foot paused in mid-stride before he turned towards one table in particular.

No one else, no human present, would ever have detected the minute hesitancy; however, Nikonar's senses thrummed to life, wondering what his master was up to. Something had definitely captured his attention.

Bale slid gracefully up to the table where Paul Peter was stationed, staring intently at paperwork in front of him while he busied himself keeping his already neat and tidy area pristine.

The dark-haired vampire reached out with one finger and tapped the table, exactly where Paul Peter's eyes were focused. Paul Peter stopped what he was doing immediately and looked up at the two beings, standing so casually yet eloquently in front of him.

Raising the finger he had just used to capture Paul Peter's attention, Bale reached slowly forward and gently caressed his nametag. Paul Peter, trying to refrain from nervously chewing on his lip, followed the slow movement of Bale's hand with his eyes, as if a hot brand were approaching his body, ready to burn a hole right through his clothing and soft skin beneath. He froze completely at the touch.

"You have a very, very sweet name," Bale told him.

Paul's eyes, which had been glued to Bale's hand, little by little rolled up to look at him. He could not speak. He could not utter a syllable, managing only a weak smile. His eyelids fluttered slightly, and although he felt cold as ice, he could feel a blush rise in his cheeks.

"Oh!" Bale said gently, pretending he was surprised. "I see you work for Delancey."

Bale pulled his hand back and observed Paul Peter dispassionately, as if he were watching a garden slug travel across a leaf.

Paul Peter nodded his head, then took a step backward and sucked in much needed air, happy to put a little distance between himself and the two impeccably attired things in front of him.

"I saw your nametag and just had to come say hello," Bale went on.

"I'm glad you did," Paul Peter managed to say, mortified at how slowly his tongue rolled around in his mouth, as if somehow a dead carp had managed to find its way in. He was sure there must be some spittle on his lips, that his errant tongue was gushing saliva down and out of his numb mouth. He shook himself like a frightened terrier trying to regain some composure and quickly looked down at the paperwork in front of him, grateful to be able to take his gaze away from Bale's face.

"Delancey is such a fine company," Bale prattled on as if he were discussing the weather. "Really, one of the most respected in the industry. You are most fortunate to be part of that agency. I'm assuming there will be more...Delancey people...actually inside, enjoying the festivities...not just out here performing menial service?"

Paul Peter stared intently at his list of invitees, laid out so carefully on the table, as he struggled to block out Bale's treacle-like voice and not take umbrage at his nasty comment. A shadow crossed over the paper as Nikonar slid their invitations onto it. The lettering seemed to swim before Paul Peter's eyes.

"Oh, ok, excellent. I see you have your invitations," Paul continued to slur.

In truth, Paul Peter barely heard him, so intent was he on getting these two signed in and on their way. He was at a loss to understand why he was so rattled and ran through in his head what he had eaten or had to drink since he had arrived. *Was he poisoned? What was happening to him?*

Reaching for a pencil, Paul Peter turned it around and used the eraser end to carefully push the invitation off his paperwork, not wanting to touch what Nikonar had just placed in front of him. The Russian seemed highly amused.

"The name of your company?" Paul asked them, struggling to maintain a professional detachment.

"Schwermut," Bale told him.

"Oh yes, of course, I see it. Ah, Schwermut, oh and, Radikale. How nice for you, umm, that you, ah, are part of two companies."

Bale watched him shaking, and the slightest smile tugged at the corner of his mouth. Nikonar noticed, of course, and was thoroughly enjoying being entertained this way! Watching Bale scare the hell out of people by just being near them was always extremely delicious.

A very nervous Paul Peter moved things mindlessly around on his table. "Ummm, Schwermut, isn't that German for... gloom?"

Nikonar barked out a short but loud laugh and took a step back, curling his finger up under his nose in a very genteel fashion as he watched this diminutive human trying to engage Bale in conversation. Tiny pinpoints of light danced merrily in his dead eyes.

Bale, raising his eyebrows, shot the Russian a quick but highly amused glance.

"Why, yes, it is. Old family name...on my mother's side," Bale lied.

Paul Peter, without looking up again, pushed their name tags toward them, then turned and stumbled away as he called over his shoulder. "Enjoy your evening...gentlemen."

Bale picked up the nametags and, without even looking at the expensive, ornately designed badges, tossed them casually into a nearby planter as he and Nikonar turned and strolled towards the party.

"Amusing little fellow, don't you think?" Nikonar commented.

Bale did not answer, which again seemed slightly odd to Nikonar, who was wondering what had his master so intrigued. Surely, not the little man from Delancey. No, whatever was holding Bale so fascinated lay somewhere inside with the fishes.

Two attendants at the massive glass doors, who would normally have looked for name tags, simply averted their eyes as they pulled open the portal, allowing Bale and Nikonar to enter.

Chapter Twelve

Frivolity and gentle laughter whirled about them as Amanda, towing Villicus behind her, waded deeply into the skillfully played music and swirling aromas from expensive perfumes, foods and liquors.

The ceiling, crafted from thick concrete and exposed metal beams that met at the top in a cleverly designed opening displaying the dark night and stars, soared high above their heads.

A simple, yet tasteful, sign that read "Checkers" was suspended above the crowd. Towards the back, where the hall opened up to a raised area flanked by tall floral arrangements, a spectacular twelve-piece orchestra deftly worked the notes of Handel's Bourree. The strings expertly flanked the subtle, flowing notes, dominated by the piano. An unusual performance for the piece, it was unique in its tone and delivery, like everything else associated with Checkers.

"Amanda. Amanda!"

Hearing her name called, Amanda looked about. Through the crowd, she saw fingers from a plump hand covered in expensive rings wiggling at her above the heads of three of the largest banking firms in Southern California. The men, these power brokers, were locked in a heated discussion, and Maggie's hand resembled a comical party favor above their neatly coiffed domes.

Laughing, Amanda moved towards the hand, again towing Villicus who seemed fascinated by everything going on around him, as he trailed along behind her. She had never been with anyone who was so interested in a power party before and kept stealing glances at him from the corner of her eye. If ever a creature belonged at an event like this, it was the stunning Villicus and he was with her.

"Amanda! There you are."

Cruising around but close enough to the bankers so they would notice her, Amanda found the person who had been hailing her.

"Maggie, oh my gosh, I was hoping you would be here."

Amanda released Villicus long enough to hug Maggie Duanes. The two women pecked each other on the cheek, almost allowing carefully lipsticked lips to brush skin before they pulled back.

"And how is it, do tell me, my dear Amanda, that you could possibly look better each time I see you?"

"Maggie! I was just wondering the same thing about you!" Amanda lied like a pro.

She took another step back and motioned for Villicus to come forward, whose mood was starting to sour with the prattle that drizzled between the two women.

"Please, Maggie, it is my pleasure to introduce you to a dear friend of mine, Villicus Shanks."

Maggie turned her heavy-lidded eyes, made up with just a touch too much teal eyeshadow, towards the impeccable Villicus who gazed down at her, his aristocratic features an impenetrable, seductive mask. Slowly, he bowed slightly at the waist and extended his hand to her, eyes locked tightly on hers.

Bobbing a discreet curtsy, carefully avoiding too much shaking of her ample body, Maggie extended her jeweled hand to Villicus and seemed to swoon as his lips gently brushed her knuckles.

"Enchanted, truly I am," Villicus whispered, his lips centimeters from the back of her hand.

Amanda smiled to herself as she watched the usually unflappable Maggie Duanes squirm.

She noticed Villicus seeming to forget his earlier annoyance with the two women and appear to take pleasure from Maggie's discomfort. Perhaps he conspiratorially enjoyed that Amanda was secretly pleased with Maggie's distress? Either way,

Amanda caught Villicus watching her from the corner of his eye. He gradually released the matronly fingers and took a step back, smiling generously at Maggie Duanes.

"Oh my," Maggie stumbled over the words. "I just, oh my. Hmmmm..."

Finally, Amanda stepped forward to rescue her friend, but Maggie gently shook her off, not wanting to break her interaction with Villicus.

"So, tell me," Maggie pressed on, regaining some of her composure now that Villicus had released her. "And how do you two know each other?"

She cast a suspicious yet friendly glance at Amanda, who felt a brief pang before explaining that Villicus was her client. Amanda pushed down hard the words that wanted to escape from her lips, the careful lie that Villicus was her lover...her man. He was not, not at all, just a client. Perhaps this evening, though, she could carefully lay the groundwork to change all of that.

Amanda felt a hot blush play across her cheeks and was grateful when the orchestra changed their quiet interlude to a splashy crescendo. She, Maggie and Villicus turned towards the musicians where her boss, J. Richmond Gaines, was pirouetting slowly in front of the orchestra. Several lights clicked on, painting him with ovals of pearl, soft blue, and baby pink, and causing multiple shadows to dance out from his swirling feet.

Hands held in front of him, palms up, J. continued to spin effortlessly around while the music, his antics and the lights hitting him drew everyone's attention. As the partygoers diverted their gaze to him, a slow wave of applause began and quickly grew as it rippled throughout the room. The orchestra, in rejoinder, built their intensity, like a religious response during some spectacular service, until everyone was engaged, their attention focused on J.

He raised his hands, curling his fingers and striking a formidable pose, much like the sorcerer subduing the pesky mops that his apprentice had let loose. With a slashing motion, he flung his arms out, and the band immediately halted. The applause that had built to a thunderous roar was replaced with cheers that quickly died down as J. nodded graciously to all in attendance.

Villicus was happy, almost giggly, as he looked at this stupendous herd in front of him. The feelings washing over him were similar to the ferocious joy and nearly feral anger that flooded his senses after his release from the flaming cathedral. These were his sheep, his personal flock.

His!

He smiled when he realized that he was absentmindedly clicking his teeth together.

Not yet, he thought to himself.

There will be plenty of time to enjoy one, maybe two of these hapless people. This could certainly turn out to be an absolutely amazing night!

Slowly, with relish, his eyes flicked over them, noting the jewels, the sumptuous materials they draped over their mortal bodies. Their veins and arteries pumped with his, not their, life force.

If only they knew what a deadly thing stood in their midst. They would learn soon enough.

Amanda stole a glance up at him, noting the expression of unbridled joy on his face, and felt a thrill steal through her. He was having a wonderful time, and she had brought him here.

Her!

"Ladies and gentlemen!" J. began, mimicking a ring announcer at a circus. "Welcome, welcome, welcome one and all to Checkers."

Another huge burst of applause sailed through the room, peppered with cheers.

J. bowed magnanimously from the waist and applauded along with them until it began to die down.

"As is our tradition, a tremendous auction has been assembled, which I invite all of you to attend."

Another barrage of lights flicked on, painting red and yellow halos on a set of doors across the room. Two young men, dressed as French coachmen with white gloves, slowly opened the door, revealing tables covered with all manner of exquisite items.

More applause resounded as J. raised his voice to mingle with it.

"Ladies and gentlemen, if you will, the silent auction awaits."

"Oooo!" Maggie squealed.

Her high-pitched retort caused Villicus to quickly turn his head and look down at her, as if some improbable cartoonish thing had startled him. Amanda laughed out loud at his reaction, then quickly covered her mouth and pretended she was actually coughing.

"What is this?" Villicus asked, still staring at Maggie, waiting for another impossible sound to erupt from her chubby throat.

"Oh! But it is too wonderful, Villicus," Maggie beamed at him. "We have a silent auction. You must come and bid on something."

"Why?" he asked quietly.

Maggie appeared confused by his question, but he was nonplussed and simply gazed quietly at her, waiting for an answer.

"Maggie, Villicus has just arrived here from Germany. He's not familiar with…"

"Oh! Well! You fill him in, my dear. I have my eye on a few things I know are in the auction."

"You go ahead, Maggie. I'll meet you in there."

Maggie nodded, all jiggly and happy, then quickly reached up and, ever so gently but inappropriately, trailed her fingers across Villicus's cheek. Mortified, Amanda watched with wide eyes, wondering what he would do, and was even more startled when Villicus quicker than she was able to really register, captured Maggie's fingers and playfully nipped at the fingertips.

Again, Maggie nearly fainted and stumbled back a step or two, almost wiping out a couple trying to squeeze past her bulk.

Villicus watched, highly amused, as Maggie bounced her way through the crowd towards the open doors, nearly knocking several people down as she plowed forward.

"I'm so sorry, Villicus. Maggie usually doesn't, I mean, she doesn't quite seem herself tonight. I've never seen her like that."

Villicus watched Amanda, taking great delight in how her lips formed the words she was speaking but not really hearing her. He did not care what she had to say. His senses were filling up with the riotous revelers pushing past him, the music, the overwhelming sea of living, breathing food sources.

And then something tugged at him.

He froze, then turned his head towards the far side of the room where the larger fish tanks stood like glorious aquatic cathedrals lit beautifully from inside, showcasing the creatures that fluttered about like glistening candy.

Amanda turned to look as well, trying to see what he was staring at.

"Villicus is everything alright?" she asked.

The orchestra began playing again, a lively rendition of the Concertino for Marimba, as party goers streamed into the auction area. Villicus walked away from her without saying a word.

Amanda watched, dumbstruck, as Villicus marched across the crowded floor. Not a soul touched him. Not even one person, in all the crush of people making their way to the auction room, so much as brushed up against him.

He disappeared from sight into a small passageway lined with enormous fish tanks.

Great, just great, Amanda thought to herself and angrily crossed her arms over her chest, wondering if she should wait for him or head into the auction.

Chiding herself, she let her arms drop to her sides and ruefully shook her head. She knew she would just wait and was not enjoying the fact that she was pandering to him. What she really wanted was Villicus doting on her, but as much she fantasized about that happening, he was a client and she ultimately, for all intents and purpose, his servant.

She found the bar and pulled herself up onto a stool. With no idea where he went, Amanda ordered a glass of wine and settled in to wait.

Chapter Thirteen

Villicus stepped into the narrow passage flanked by enormous tanks that glowed and bubbled from their aeration systems. Turning his head slightly, he saw the thick, toothy, underslung jaw of a wolf eel, pumping slowly, as it gazed at him from its aquatic world.

The passageway was actually quite dark, the only light nearby focused inside the tanks. Sensing the tons of water pressing against the thick glass, Villicus was amazed at a flashback that struck him hard. A memory of the days upon days he spent suffocating beneath the massive tonnage of the cathedral that surrounded him, howling like a wounded animal in rage against his tormentors.

It was not anxiety he felt, for that emotion did not transfer from his human self to his vampire being. It was not fear either, for that, too, did not survive. Was it a remnant, some raw memory he allowed to live in his mind, as fuel for his rage? Yes, rage indeed, that was part of what made up Villicus Shanks, one of the few, raw, human emotions that survived the transition to his vampire self.

Taking a few more steps into the darkened passage, Villicus froze once again. Something else, something more deadly than the fearsome wolf eel, was near him.

Quietly, without fanfare, Bale spoke from behind him.

"Lovely woman you are with tonight, Villicus. Truly, most exquisite, like a rare jewel. Planning on ripping her throat out later?"

Villicus spun about, graceful but vampire quick, and studied the two figures before him. Bale and Nikonar emerged from the shadows.

"That's no way to greet an old friend," Nikonar chided Bale.

"Friend?" Villicus hissed.

The enormous Russian walked closer to Villicus staring at him in amazement.

"You survived," he whispered, unable to disguise the awe and what sounded like a touch of admiration in his voice.

"No thanks to you."

"It wasn't my idea to imprison you—"

"He's right," Bale cut him off. "It was mine."

Bale stepped up to Villicus just inches from his face. Villicus felt himself quivering in spite of the loathing he felt for his maker.

"I'm surprised to see you, Villicus. How did you manage to survive?"

"What do you care?"

"Oh, I care. I care a lot. I was wondering who was sneaking around these days, all the attacks on my companies, on me! Those little hints of aggression, duplicitous, thieving, just like you..."

"It's just a game, Bale," Villicus interjected. "Always has been. Just something to do to keep from getting bored while we feed off of...them. The more money we control, the more we control...them. You taught me that, or did you forget?"

Bale observed him coolly for a moment, seemingly not terribly threatened by him, more curious actually. This was obviously an adjustment for him, something new to take in and understand.

"What do you want, Villicus?" he asked patiently.

"From you? Nothing. The world is big enough these days for both of us."

"So then tell me," Bale whispered. "Of all the places in this big world, why are you here?"

Chapter Fourteen

Amanda, having abandoned her wine and the bar, wandered around the area, trying nonchalantly to spot Villicus. *Where had he gone to?*

She raised up a bit on her toes, trying to catch a glimpse of him.

Suddenly, arms wrapped quickly around her waist, and someone kissed the back of her neck.

"Villicus! What are you—" she exclaimed happily, then rushed forward out of the embrace with disgust when she realized Mark Hadley was her captor.

Swaying in front of her, Mark glared at her through lit eyes, seeping with anger, lust and too much twelve-year-old scotch.

"Don't do that," he hissed and slurred at her.

"Mark, what are you doing?" Amanda demanded.

"I just wanted to say hi. So, who's your boyfriend?"

"None of your business. He's just a friend."

Aware that he was quite drunk, Amanda turned and moved away from him, but Hadley followed quickly, kicking the back of her feet as he lurched forward in his inebriated state.

"Don't walk away from me!" he yelled, grabbing her arm hard and yanking her back towards him.

"Stop it. Leave me alone!"

"You mean it? You mean it! What are you going to do? Where's your boyfriend now, that hulking fucktard? Huh? Where is he?"

"Stop it! Let me go!"

"Are you fucking him? Huh? Is he a good fuck, Amanda? Does he have a big dick?"

"Mark, you need to stop this right now." Amanda pleaded with him as she struggled to pull from his grasp.

"You and I should be fucking," he ranted on, barely audible over the music. "I have a big dick, you know. You'd love it."

"What?!"

Hadley shouted to be heard over the band.

"I said, I have a big dick!"

The band leader, seeing the altercation between Hadley and Amanda, cued the musicians to stop playing just as Hadley had shouted the last sentence to her. All of those still in the area, including J., stared in stunned silence at the drunken, reeling Hadley.

Quickly, quietly and with deadly focus, Villicus walked up behind Hadley and peeled him away from Amanda with one hand, then tossed him several feet across the room. Hadley landed near the feet of J., who helped him awkwardly up. Shoving him away as soon as he was upright, Hadley nearly pitched over backwards in his drunken state.

"Listen, old man," J. admonished Hadley, "just what the hell is going on?"

"Fuck you!" Hadley shouted at him as he turned and shoved his way staggeringly towards the exit past startled party goers.

Like the cliché'd damsel in distress, Amanda waited to one side, wringing her hands. She snapped her head back and forth, watching Hadley and then turning to observe what Villicus might do next.

Villicus stood quietly just inside a ring of light, the beams above giving him a soft, glowing halo. With his head tilted down slightly, he watched Hadley's awkward exit. Amanda wanted to rush over to him, but stood back, not sure if it was from fear or awe.

A twitter of high-pitched conversation rippled through the room as the other guests regained their composure. J. made his way to Amanda and gently placed a hand on her upper arm.

"Amanda, my God! Are you alright?"

She quickly nodded her head that she was.

Feeling flushed from the adrenaline rush of the moment, she was more than a bit awestruck at how easily Villicus had tossed Mark aside—something she wished she could have done herself many times. Taking a few deep breaths, Amanda looked away from Herr Shanks as she tried to compose herself.

Villicus stopped directly in front of her and crooked a finger under her chin, then gently tilted her face up towards his.

"And you?" he asked.

Amanda trembled from his touch, and her first instinct was to dissolve into tears. She owed herself the breakdown. After all, that miscreant Mark Hadley had tried to oil his way into her life over and over again.

One of the musicians nearby quietly tested the strings on his violin, and that gentle plucking sound caused her to look over in that direction. She saw the dozens of party goers staring at her and noticed many of them whispering to each other, trying to hide their mouths behind jeweled and manicured hands.

Oh no, she thought to herself, dredging up the tougher steel she was made of and turning back to Villicus. "Not in front of this crowd"

Wrapping her hand around his, she pulled his curved fingers away and gave them a firm but friendly shake.

"Fine, Villicus, I'm just fine. Thank you, for stepping in and…," she stumbled over the right words to say.

Villicus quickly flipped her hand over and kissed the back just as Paul Peter quietly, but quickly, stepped to her side.

Carefully eyeing Villicus he whispered to her, "You okay?"

"Yup."

"What happened?"

"Oh, he was just drunk."

Paul Peter looked at a fuming J. Richmond Gaines angrily talking to some of his Delancey toadies.

"I think he was just fired, too. You sure you're okay?"

"Not to worry," Villicus announced to him. "I will look after her."

"Yes, I can see that."

Chapter Fifteen

Paul Peter headed back into the foyer, anxious to gather up his papers and head home. He had had enough of Checkers for one night and knew that Amanda, now that Hadley was gone and she was on the arm of her German prince, was going to rally and shine brighter than she ever had before.

The lights in the reception area had been dimmed to allow the party lights to be the dominant feature inside the aquarium. Several tanks lined the space, their aerators creating a soothing, white noise. A few people wandered quietly around the area, workers finishing up paperwork and starting to pack up some of the things in the reception area.

Humming to himself, happy that his boss was not only having a good time but that her nemesis, that squirmy toad Hadley, had just shot himself in the foot, Paul Peter giggled, actually visualizing this happening. So caught up in his fantasy, picturing Hadley jumping around on one foot and swearing a blue streak with smoke pouring from the toe of his expensive handmade shoe, that he was unaware someone was standing quite close to him. Bumping forcefully into a body as he turned, Paul Peter startled and jumped backwards.

"Oh my God, I'm so sorry, are you...?" his words trailed off.

Standing before him was Bale, stock-still, with one hand elegantly resting in his jacket pocket.

"That was some ruckus. Anything the matter?" Bale asked quickly, but quietly.

"No, no. Ruckus all gone."

Pointing back into the main room, swirling with colorful lights and animated party goers, Paul Peter indicated Amanda happily chattering now with her friend Maggie, Villicus planted stoically nearby.

"Who is she?"

"She is my boss. Amanda Brax."

"Oh right, Ms. Brax. Your boss, is she now? Very talented lady at..."

Paul Peter points to his name tag showing the Delancey name and logo.

"Delancey."

Lying artfully, Bale continued to toy with Paul Peter, "Yes, I have heard of her. She's been handling the accounts for...Mr. Shanks is it?"

"I'm sorry, but I can't say."

"No, of course not. Privileged information, and all that."

Bale took a small step closer towards Paul Peter and leaned in, smelling his neck.

"I do like that cologne," he prattled on, "What's it called?"

Beginning to stammer badly, Paul Peter managed to tell him, "I don't remember."

Feeling trapped and frightened but not clearly understanding why, Paul Peter turned on his heel and ran from the reception area. Bale smiled slyly and, pulling his hand from his pocket to smooth his perfect hair back, sauntered off after him.

Further back in the room, hidden deeply in the shadows, Nikonar watched his master playing with his meal for the evening. Instead of following him out to perhaps enjoy the kill with him, he headed back into the party and found his way to Villicus.

The crowds of people, plied with liquor, were becoming more animated, chattering excitedly about the upcoming auction. As if on cue, like a carefully choreographed dance, they scurried out of the way of Nikonar as the elegant beast made his way unhindered through their midst. Arriving in front of Amanda, she shook her head then batted her eyes several times, equally startled and enamored by his appearance.

"Good evening," he said, his words, delicately laced with his Russian inflection and seductive tone.

"Hello," Amanda whispered to him, mesmerized by his euphoric gaze, for just a split second forgetting that Villicus was still right by her side.

Reluctantly, Villicus introduced him.

"Amanda, this is Nikonar Federov."

"Oh," she gushed, reluctant to look away from the tall Russian. "You two know each other?"

"Yes, very old friends," Nikonar purred at her.

Bouncing happily up to them, Maggie chirped brightly, "The auction is about to start! Better hurry before all the good bargains are gone."

"Oh great," Amanda told her, somewhat annoyed at her bad timing, "We'll be right in."

Villicus leaned down to speak to her. "You go ahead. I'll follow you in a moment."

Startled, Amanda had not seen him move, yet there he was, planted firmly in front of that most delicious Russian fellow, blocking her view. She tried to look around him, to capture that gaze again, but Villicus caught her under the chin with his finger and forced her to look at him. With his free hand, he reached out without looking and caught Maggie by the wrist, pulling her close.

"You ladies need to go now. I will join you later."

Maggie, quite tipsy, giggled loudly and grabbed Amanda, fairly pulling her off her feet as they tottered off to the other room where the auction was being held.

"You heard your darling little schnitzel! Come on!" Maggie gushed.

Quickly, they folded into the stream of people heading in. Just before they passed through the doors being held open for them, he saw her turn to look anxiously back at him.

And then she was gone.

But she had looked back for him.

Villicus stared after her, truly surprised that he was glad she had looked back. There was something about this woman that he could not quite explain, let alone his odd feelings and behavior when he was around her.

"I had hoped you would let me explain," Nikonar said.

Turning about, Villicus responded, "You were never that articulate."

"Just look around you, at the greed, the opulence. See how these humans have flourished under our guidance..."

"Your manipulation."

"Call it what you will. You are the same as us, Villicus. You had the same lust for the avarice and the domination of people when we met you. You begged to be one of us..."

Feeling his eyes flashing black, Villicus shoved Nikonar, teeth bared.

"Do you have any idea what it was like? All those years, centuries that I sat in the dark praying for a death that wouldn't come."

"Villicus, the times were very hard for us. Surely you remember. The plague was ravaging Europe. Barely enough to feed off of those puss riddled corpses. There were more wolves than people! We were starving! Wars between our kind were inevitable. Bale felt threatened by you, and he could have killed you, but he didn't!"

"Maybe he should have when he had the chance. Why didn't you come back for me?"

"I don't know. I...I didn't think you would..."

"...still exist? You're a pawn, Nikonar. Bale plays you like a fiddle. Tell me, what does it feel like to be so subservient to such a piece of trash? Maybe I had it better than you."

"Don't say that. I was there when you joined us!"

"Did I forget to say thank you?"

Seething with anger now, Villicus took a forceful step toward Nikonar and was shocked to see him back fearfully away. Disgusted, Villicus turned from him and entered the auction.

Nikonar was left behind, staring at his back. He watched Villicus walk away, unsure whether to follow him or not, but soon realized that any further exchange between them tonight would be pointless.

Once, they had considered each other friends of a sort. At least, as friendly as violent, aggressive monsters might be. One of the things Nikonar had come to enjoy through the decades is

being at a group slaying, where more than one vampire attacked
and leveled a group of humans. His mind wandered back.

Usually, it would be on board a ship which they would then
scuttle so that the vessel and its dead inhabitants drifted to the
bottom of the sea, obscuring all of their sins. During one such
outing, another vampire made the comment that they were
performing a needed service, feeding the fish and providing an
entire ship that would eventually turn into a magnificent reef.

"But, exactly, of course we are performing a magnificent
service," Nikonar boasted.

"What is the word the humans use?" one of them asked.

"Preservationist, I do believe."

The group of them, five in all during this outing, howled
and laughed at the joke. If any word could be used to describe a
vampire, it would not be a preservationist.

The mood was so high between all of them that they decided
to sink another one and found an exquisite, tall ship harbored
not far down the coast.

Nonchalantly, the five of them walked up the gang plank
until they were on board. Their presence at first startled the
sailors who were not sure what was going on. These vampires
were attired in modern attire, resplendent with jewelry and, for
some of them, expensive, beautifully designed hats and walking
sticks topped with gold and large gems.

It was the early 1900s and the vampires, along with enjoying
the vast numbers of their herds all around the world, got a great
deal of pleasure making money from the fascinating technology
that was taking such a hold on people and their lives.

It was getting late and the moon was quite high in the
sky. The deck of the ship was alight with several torches and
a couple of incandescent lights that, unlike the torches which
created soft, appealing shadows, the bulbs starkly lit the areas
around them and created ugly, hard edged shadows. It was an
unpleasant contrast.

One of the sailors ran to get the captain and the other officers.
They did not know who these people were but assumed, by the
way they were dressed, that they were important and probably
there to see the captain.

The captain dashed out of the quarterdeck, struggling to get into his coat as he hustled along. His officers, likewise wrestling with their uniforms to make themselves presentable, were right on his heels.

"Gentlemen. Hello," the captain said, walking briskly towards them with his hand extended. "How may I be of service?"

Nikonar, the largest in this group, stepped forward and offered to shake hands. As soon as the captain placed his hand in the firm grasp of the massive Russian vampire standing before him, he knew something was seriously wrong. The feeling of those cold, dead fingers wrapping around his turned his stomach.

The captain had to really struggle to avoid throwing up all over the deck.

Shock and surprise caused him to stammer. He tried to withdraw his hand, but Nikonar would not let go. The captain looked puzzled at first, trying to understand what was happening. He looked up into the Russian's stony face becoming even more confused by his sickening smile. With as much strength as he could muster, he tried to pull his hand free, but was not able.

He smashed the back of Nikonar's hand and attempted to pry his fingers up, but the vampire stood there, frozen to the spot, unmoving. His eyes, like black fire, focused on the man who was fighting to break free.

This was highly amusing for himself and his comrades, so he did not let go.

The officers stepped forward, extremely confused, but seeing that their captain was in trouble, they did their best to help. Nikonar grabbed the first one who stepped forward with a wooden pin to smash his hand, and with his free hand, slowly turned the man's head around so he was looking backward.

His eyes blinked frantically before his life drifted sadly away. The sailors, clustered behind their captain, panicked. Some crossed themselves while others threw themselves overboard and swam for the shore, only to find themselves face to face with one of the vampires who had witnessed their attempted escape.

Their screams, drifting across the water to the ship, were devastating.

Nikonar had learned over the many years he had stalked the planet that although he and his kind sometimes gathered together, it took very little for them to turn on each other. Truly, loyalty was non-existent. After all, what was the point of friendship between any of them when they could simply take whatever they wanted, whenever they wanted, and never needed permission from anyone to do as they pleased?

It did not take long for their hunting party to dissolve into a snarling, brutal melee. Two of the vampires collided when they both went after the same victim. The hapless sailor had dropped to the deck when he saw them headed for him. As the vicious fight raged above him, he crawled away and hid himself below deck.

So much for their second outing that evening. Instead of slaughtering an entire crew then scuttling their pretty ship, half of the crew escaped, in shock, after having watched their captain, officers and fellow sailors literally ripped to pieces. The ship of course was visited by the authorities and curious residents when several of the sailors who had managed to get away tried to convince them of what happened.

One look at the ship, with pools of blood still coagulating on the deck and pieces of the captain and crew strewn about, was enough to convince anyone that something truly horrifying and paranormal had happened there. Another story now about the vampires started circulating. Because of their stupidity and infighting, these secretive creatures were further exposed to the populace. Nikonar left the ship the moment the fight broke out and watched these idiots ruin what would have otherwise been a very pleasant evening.

He certainly had no feelings for Villicus and none for Bale either. Bale was his maker, so he paid homage to him, but he was part of a much older race than the mere vampires whom they had helped to spawn. Bale was otherworldly. He, unlike Nikonar or Villicus had never been human at all. He was as he had always been.

A Nephelim.

A small smile caused the corners of his mouth to curl. If Bale was part of that bastard breed created by angels copulating with mortal women, then he never had a soul. The smile quickly broadened, and soon Nikonar was laughing loudly. This revelation, the first he had had in over a hundred years, was mind bending for him and brought him back to the present. Could it be true?

He sat down on the edge of a tank which held small rays and turtles that children could hold and pet during their visits to the aquarium. Staring into the water, watching ripples form as the small creatures sputtered about in their watery world, Nikonar placed both hands over his chest and closed his eyes. He knew his delicate fingers would not detect the beating of a heart, for his had died a long time ago.

What, though, had become of his soul? Had it died along with his heart?

Nikonar did not think so and would now ponder this question for decades, trying to puzzle out an answer.

Abruptly aware that a beautiful, raven-haired woman was staring at him from across the room, he rose and was beside her, crossing the expanse between them much faster than she could detect. Startled, she rose quickly and backed away, knocking over a small bus table covered with expensive crystal glasses and small china plates. The place settings hit the concrete floor, shattering into thousands of glinting shards that flew in all directions.

Nikonar pressed forward, leaning into her until their faces were just centimeters apart. He was aware of her breath on his face and loved the feeling. So much life in this one.

He was about to snuff it out when he became aware that his maker, that piece of shit Nephelim whom he hated and loved equally, was preparing to kill nearby. Nikonar so enjoyed watching him work.

Delicately, he kissed the woman ever-so-gently on her lips, then turned and was gone so quickly, he seemed to have vanished before her eyes. She fainted into a heap on the ground, surrounded by a twinkling sea of porcelain and glass.

Evening had brought the moon high into the sky, and Paul Peter was just able to catch glimpses of it as he stumbled through the foliage surrounding the back of the aquarium. He could see the building; it was hard to miss, perched like some enormous gray whale in the hills, but in his panic, he was not sure how to get down to the parking lot. His car was there, with lights, people and those helpful valets who would bring his car to him and elegantly hold the door open so he could jump in and race off into the city.

Well, not race exactly. Paul Peter drove like a little old lady and never exceeded the speed limit.

The hillside was getting steeper and again, as had happened several times already, his feet flew out from under him, causing him to fall hard onto the grass and slide for several feet. His suit was covered in dirt and pine needles, and he was aware that the few papers he had managed to hold on to before he fled the aquarium were fluttering down the hill below him. The grass was getting quite damp in the evening air, and some of the sheets of paper, he saw, were stuck to the grass or molding themselves around the trunks of the pine trees.

What the hell was he doing here? How did he get up here?

Staggering back to his feet, pulling grass and twigs from his hair, he grasped some lower branches on the trees to help steady himself. He was aware that he was shaking badly, and his breath was coming in and out of his body in ragged gasps. Holding tightly to a branch on this steep hillside, he looked about and saw more lights down and to his right. That must be the parking lot.

Slowly, he turned, getting ready to slide down the hill towards that glowing, beckoning haven. Just as he finished his turn, Paul Peter found himself face to face with Bale, who, still dressed impeccably, caught him around the wrist just as he let go of the branch. Paul Peter expected both of them to tumble down the steep hillside, but they were frozen there, on the hill, with the tantalizing lights down below backlighting Bale. He looked like a silhouette with blazing eyes.

"I want you to tell me about Ms. Brax. She certainly seems to have captured Herr Shank's fancy. Tell me."

"Who? You what?"

"Your boss, Ms. Brax. What hold does she have over our mutual German friend?"

Paul Peter tried to pull free from Bale's grasp, but it would have been easier to free his arm from set cement. Bale reached up with his free hand and gently stroked Paul Peter's face, flicking dirt and bits of grass that had become stuck to his cheek. As the dead, cold fingers scraped across his skin, Paul Peter became aware again, aware of why he had run up onto the hillside and into the trees. He was a mouse facing a rattlesnake, and the terror that had caused him to run in a blind panic began to creep up on him again. He felt faint coming on.

Bale thwacked him on the nose, getting his attention.

"I'm being most patient, wouldn't you agree?"

"What? What do you want to know?"

"Everything."

"Please don't hurt me!"

Paul Peter, twisting and pulling hard, was doing all he could to free himself from Bale's grasp. In desperation, he bit down on Bale's fingers. Outraged at the puny human's attempt to free himself, Bale shook him like a terrier might shake a rat and threw him into the trees.

Hitting the trunk hard, Paul Peter bit down on his tongue and could feel a piece of it slice away. His mouth filled with blood, and as hard as it had been before to breathe, it was becoming next to impossible now. Full terror gripped him as he tried to run, but the hill was too steep. He fell and started to plummet down the steep grade.

Bale caught him part way down the hill and lifted him off his feet by the hair on his head. The pain was immense, and Paul Peter started to scream, spraying Bale's face and flawless suit with blood and dirt.

Fully enraged now, Bale held onto Paul Peter's hair and then swung his body about, slamming it into the trees. His bones cracked and sounded like gunfire echoing off the hillside. Finally, Bale threw him out into space, and Paul Peter's body dropped a good thirty feet before it met the angle of the hill and came to rest at the base of some large boulders near the bottom, right beside the parking lot.

Chapter Sixteen

Mark Hadley, after storming out of the party, stomped up to the valet's station and pawed through the keys hanging neatly on their rack until he found the ones for his car. The brave little valets tried several times to stop him, but he threw the other keys around, causing them to scurry and find them in the grass and ornate gardens.

One of the valets tore after him, trying desperately to stop him, telling him he had maybe 'sipped a bit too much' at the party. Hadley snatched up a sign with an arrow pointing towards the valet station and threatened to bash him with it. Ducking the possible blow and aware that this drunken man in front of him was too much for him to try to stop, the valet retreated back to where the others were gathering up the strewn keys and called the police.

Hadley jumped into his car, a renovated 1972 Porsche, black with a thick yellow stripe down the side, and turned the engine over. Putting the car in reverse, he saw that a large Bentley was blocking his escape. The pain-in-the-ass little valets had stacked many of the cars this way to maximize where to put them during the party. Putting the car in gear, Hadley drove up onto the lawn and ripped through the garden, tearing out part of the sign covered in photos and text explaining what the flowers were that he had just destroyed.

The car was approaching sixty miles per hour as he fishtailed all over the lawn. Hitting the asphalt, he nearly spun it completely around but bounced it off the edge of a hill that butted up against the drive. Terrified and angry at the same time, he did not let up on the gas and instead kept fighting with the car, working through the fishtailing until he was moving forward in a straight line.

The driveway swerved uphill until it met the main drive for the big park where the aquarium was located. His Porsche became airborne for a split second as the main road dropped down and to the left, towards Los Angeles. Mark, for a moment, thought he had done something really stupid and was going to die when the car met the pavement again and rocketed down at a rather steep angle, but as soon as the tires hit the ground, he actually had remarkable control over the fast-moving vehicle.

Laughing out loud, he reached up with one hand and patted the dashboard.

"German engineering!"

Remembering that Amanda, his Amanda, was back at the party with that German prick, he screamed, "Fuck the Germans and their fucking engineering!"

Hadley slowed the car a bit as he hit the city streets, still fuming over the events of the evening. Cruising down Century Blvd., he could see the large, neon sign for the Delancey group up by Sunset Blvd. A wide grin split his face, and Hadley drove like a poster boy for auto safety, all the way to the building. He was forming a plan and did not want LA's finest to pull him over.

Moments later, he was in the building, having parked his car in J. Richmond Gaines private spot right next to the elevator.

"Yeah, and fuck you, too, J."

Still drunk and furious, he got into the elevator and keyed in a code allowing him access to the floor where his office was. The Muzak played a seriously creepy version of "Memories". Hadley took his shoe off and bashed the speaker to pieces.

After arriving at his floor, he exited the elevator, one shoe on and the other left jammed into the speaker. Stomping across the wide expanse of the reception area, he flew into his office and fired up his computer.

He dropped heavily into a chair, just as the computer monitor flickered to life. Looking through several folders, he started keying in access codes, viewing page after page of confidential files.

"Amanda...Amanda," he hissed, actually starting to laugh a bit. "You wouldn't fuck me, no matter how nicely I asked, ya dumb bitch. Well, I'm gonna fuck you now, and I hope you like it."

Chapter Seventeen

The auction at the aquarium ended, and the guests chattered happily, comparing things they had purchased for extraordinary sums of money. Amanda and Villicus headed out with them towards the lobby. Smiling broadly, she cradled a small bag in one hand.

Heading to the Delancey table, Amanda asked one of the people still working there if Paul Peter was still about.

"No, no, haven't seen him in quite a while. I think he may have left already."

"Ahh, thanks," she said to the worker, sounding disappointed, then turned to Villicus and told him, "Darn! I wanted to show him this."

Eying the bag, he asked, "What is it?"

"You'll see!" she smiled wickedly.

With her arm through his, Amanda and Villicus headed out towards the parking lot. They drove away, unaware that Paul Peter's body lay by the large, ornate boulders at the edge of the parking lot.

Bale and Nikonar watched them cruise out of the parking lot, cars stopping to let them pass.

Quickly, quietly, nearly imperceptibly, Bale nodded his head towards Nikonar, who became one with the shadows and reluctantly disappeared, flash quick, into the night.

Chapter Eighteen

Laughing, silly, and inebriated from more than the wine she had enjoyed that evening, Amanda keyed open the door to her home and trotted inside. Pausing a step or two inside, she turned to look at Villicus standing just beyond the threshold, watching her quietly, holding the key to his car in his fingers. His head tilted to one side as he observed her.

Amanda held the bag out to him, dangling it delicately from one finger.

"You must come inside to see what I bought for you."

"Must I?" he asked, slightly amused by her antics.

Giggling, she waggled the bag at him again, then quickly reached out and grabbed his car keys before turning and dashing into her living room.

Villicus entered and closed the door behind him, aware that she was turning on dimming lights on in the other room. From hidden recesses, soft music washed the air.

Turning a corner, he stepped down into the room and saw her curled up on the sofa. Her shoes lay on the floor, pushed out of the way under her coffee table. Her head lay in her hand, and she looked up at him, a small smile played about her lips. On the couch beside her sat the bag. Amanda lifted it up and patted the seat next to her, inviting him to sit down.

Villicus accepted the offer, and no sooner had he landed on the soft fabric than Amanda quickly hoisted herself up and slid into his lap. She held the bag out for him in one hand, his keys in the other.

"Which one do you want first?" she said.

Her speech was slurred somewhat, but her intentions were

clear. She certainly wanted Herr Shanks to spend the night. Gently, Villicus teased the car keys from her.

"Oh rats, well ok."

Amanda was disappointed he wanted his keys back so quickly but thought perhaps he just wanted them so they did not get lost.

The vision in her head of them getting eaten up by the couch while she and Villicus tumbled about was simultaneously making her laugh and turning her on at the same time. She wiggled around a bit on his lap, hoping to make her intentions crystal clear.

Amanda held up the bag.

"Here...I got this for you at the auction."

Gently, he tugged the bag from her hand and carefully removed a small tissue wrapped object. Peeling the paper away revealed a small, German wind-up-toy—a tiny glockenspiel, crafted with great precision and attention to detail. It appeared to be at least a hundred years old, if not older.

Carefully, he wound it up and set it on the table before them, and together they watched the silly thing go through its paces.

"Do you like it?" she asked.

"Yes. It reminds me of home."

Amanda stared deeply into his eyes, then leaned forward and wrapped her arms tightly about his neck. Villicus arms at first remained at his side until, slowly, he brought them up around her.

Taking the movement of his arms as a cue, she kissed him, long and deep. Villicus did not react. In fact, his arms fell back down by his side. Frustrated, she pulled away.

"You don't like me," she said, clearly disappointed.

"I do."

"You don't show it."

"I know. I'm trying to figure out how."

"What is that supposed to mean?"

Tears glistened in the corners of her eyes. Angry, sad, and beginning to feel embarrassed, she turned her face away from his. Gently, he stroked her cheek, and immediately she felt turned on by him again. Under his touch, she felt incredibly aroused and gave in completely to the sweet drive that allowed her to push all feelings of frustration and embarrassment aside. Nuzzling his neck, her warm breath gushed out, deep and heavy. She nibbled at his ear and neck, then grabbed his ponytail and tugged it gently at first, then forcefully.

Sensing her growing ardor, Villicus closed his eyes and tried to imagine what she was feeling. Gently stroking her throat with his fingertips, he whispered in her ear, "Do you like that?"

Amanda felt intoxicated from his touch and slurred her response. Her words were unintelligible; however, Villicus knew exactly what she meant to say by the way her lower lip quivered. Her eyelids fluttered delicately, and Villicus could see that her eyes were rolled back into her head. His need to take her, to take her life, began to rise like a black tide pushing the light away.

In her altered state, she pitched forward and pushed her face hard against his neck, her heated breath puffing out raggedly against his pearly, lifeless skin. Villicus could feel his face transform. His head tilted slowly back as his lower jaw dropped open, stretching the skin on his cheeks until the flesh look ready to tear.

Amanda moaned and struggled to pull herself upright so she could look into his face, but Villicus held her tightly against his chest, squeezing so hard to keep her prisoner that it was difficult for her to breathe. This perilous embrace added to her intoxicated state, because she was barely able to get enough oxygen.

She wrapped the long tail of his hair around her hand tightly to anchor his head, then pulled until it tilted back. Completely overwhelmed by his power, unaware of why her libido raged out of control and not caring about it, she kissed Villicus deeply. Pushing his mouth open with her own, Amanda flicked her tongue into his mouth.

Easing up, Villicus placed both of his large hands, with fingers splayed widely, across her back and marveled at the rush of blood pushing through the capillaries just under the surface. Gently, with a feather touch, he traced their source back to larger vessels that disappeared deeply into her body.

The darkness was clouding his mind, pinching and closing off any sense of his human guise that he used with the herds, that of the graceful German lord who thrilled those around him. A monster was emerging, and the need to kill her was getting harder to control. He had to stop, to stop her, before her life was gone. Villicus did not want her dead right now. He actually was thinking that maybe he never wanted her dead.

This epiphany, that he actually felt compassion for a human, startled and rattled Villicus. It was something new, or perhaps something very old from his previous life? His eyes, those soulless black wells, quickly reverted back to his human guise and he grasped Amanda by the shoulders, pushing her away from him.

He could see her face, slack and appearing drunk from the power he exerted over her. Any inebriation she had been experiencing from the wine she drank had been greatly usurped by his dominance. Gently, for fear of crushing her, he slid his hands down to her upper arms and used just his fingertips to slide her onto the couch next to him.

Vampire quick, Villicus rose and, after scooping up the little glockenspiel, said to her, "Thank you again for the beautiful gift."

Amanda, dazed and disheveled, her make-up smeared across her face, looked up at him, trying to get her bearings. In her stupor, he appeared to float before her. She blinked her eyes once, and he was gone.

Chapter Nineteen

Well past midnight, downtown Los Angeles was virtually a ghost town. Flitting wisps of tattered newspapers blew through intersections where a handful of cars sped along the asphalt. Several drivers ignored red streetlights as they darted recklessly across.

Villicus sat in his car, the headlights and engine turned off, as he stared up at the Delancey building. Several lights burned brightly up on the 10th floor, and with his amazing eyes, he was able to see a form moving about inside. A human form.

He flicked on his cell phone and smiled as the unit powered up with its slick, animated, brightly colored opening. The more he played with the phone, the more the little things it could do entertained him so. Even though he did not need to turn the phone off each time he used it, he did anyway, just to watch the phone go through its flashy startup.

He clicked on one of the two contacts he had saved in the device and waited patiently as it rang across town.

"What?!" Howley Bennet shouted into the phone, struggling to be heard above the screams and roars coming from his latest slasher flick, Switchblade Rex, a violent Tyrannosaurus Rex-themed gore fest.

A bit taken aback, Villicus paused then said, "Howley, it is I. Villicus."

"Yeah, I know!" Howley shouted again, annoyed at being bothered.

Villicus listened intently to the shrieks and howls coming through the phone like compressed bullets of sound. Overwhelmed, not sure what was going on, he listened a bit longer without speaking, trying to understand what he was hearing.

"Villicus! I know it's you. Dude, what's up?" Howley shouted. Villicus was fascinated with his colloquialisms. For a vampire, Howley surely was well-adapted to the modern environment. Villicus felt like a museum piece, sitting in his dark Ferrari, his tuxedo still crisp and immaculate. The small car felt like a coffin on wheels.

He watched a streetlight change to red a block away, and then turned his head to follow five bright green Suzuki Hayabusas, one after the other, flying illegally through the intersection, their riders all wearing shiny black helmets with blackened face plates to preserve their anonymity. The sound of the engines sounded like gigantic, annoying insects to him. If he did not have a different agenda for the evening, he would drive after the five cyclists and kill them all.

He knew Howley was still waiting for him.

"I humbly beseech your assistance." Villicus said quietly.

Villicus listened to the screams and roars for a few more seconds, then silence, as Howley terminated the call. He knew he was on his way and waited quietly in the dark, watching the shrouded city streets for any further signs of life.

Mark Hadley, less drunk than when he arrived but none the less deranged and stupid in his rage, stormed about Amanda's office with one shoe off and one shoe on. Just moments ago, he had kicked the door open and stomped through the room, smashing everything he could get his hands on. He loved doing this. For each object he smashed, he pictured in his mind's eye that it was her face.

He was oblivious to the city spread out for miles and miles outside this high perch and slammed drawers open and closed, spewing paper clips, memo pads and post-a-notes all about.

Finally, he found what he was looking for. Reaching back into a drawer he had just slammed shut but had drifted open again, he spied a small, purple book. Pulling it out, he quickly thumbed through and actually made a gleeful, chortling sound as he tumbled into her chair.

Turning on her computer, he began to key in numbers and letters, and after entering the final one from this purple book with a flourish, he hit enter. The monitor shifted colors and patterns as a new site came to life. Suddenly, row after row of encrypted data solved itself, and he stared intently at the private, encoded files of Amanda Brax.

"Ha!" he shouted triumphantly. "Ha! Oh, this is great! Amanda, you are going to be so screwed when the Securities Commission looks at what I'm going to do to you. I'm going to enjoy visiting you in prison, you nasty little bitch!"

Quickly, Hadley started to shift dollar amounts and dates of transactions around. He copied key parts of the ledger and pasted it into an email for J. Richmond Gaines. A split second after he hit send, a huge hand flew past his head and smashed the monitor into confetti.

"What the fuck!" he hollered.

Villicus spun him around in his chair and leaned in close, their faces just centimeters apart.

"What the fuck are you doing here?" Hadley demanded.

Patiently, and with measured diction, Villicus said to him, "You need to improve your vocabulary."

Vampire quick, Villicus tore Hadley's tie off and quickly bound his arms behind his back. Stunned, Hadley could not quite figure out what was happening to him.

"What are you doing? I'll have you arrested. You and that fucking bitch of yours. She is going to pay! I'll make both of you pay!"

Villicus shoved the wheeled office chair, sending Hadley out into the hall with such force that he hit a large, decorative planter, causing greenery and dirt to rain all about. The impact had stunned Hadley, and he shook his head, trying to clear it.

Villicus spun him about again and then propelled him down the hallway.

"Untie me now, mother fucker!"

His outburst made Villicus laugh.

"No, I don't think so...mother fucker."

As they moved past a cluster of desks the traders' secretaries used, Villicus grabbed a stuffed fabric frog from the top of a filing cabinet and jammed it into Hadley's mouth, letting the legs hang down over his quivering chin. Hadley shook his head violently but could not dislodge it.

They approached a bank of elevators, and Villicus pushed the up button.

A few moments later, one of the richly appointed elevator cars swooshed open its doors, and Villicus wheeled Hadley inside. A Muzak version of the Archies "Sugar, Sugar" dribbled from the speakers. Villicus punched the highest floor number, and quickly they were underway.

They arrived on the top floor, and Villicus maneuvered the bound Hadley through a maze of mostly unused hallways. Dragging the chair behind him, he thumped him up a short stairway to the roof entrance where he found the door, of course, locked. Villicus gave it a good kick. It not only flew open; it exploded off its hinges and landed with a loud thud several feet away on the composite roof.

Villicus grabbed the back of Hadley's chair and chucked him through the open doorway, sending him airborne a good thirty feet before he landed and skidded to a halt on the gritty surface. Striding quickly up behind him, Villicus hoisted the chair effortlessly in the air again with one hand and carried the struggling Hadley to the edge of the building.

Hadley's eyes opened even wider in terror when he saw a figure standing nonchalantly on the edge. It was Howley. Villicus dropped the chair down on the edge about fifteen feet from Howley, then sat down next to it.

"This is Mark. Say hello, Mark." Villicus said.

With one finger, he pushed the chair rapidly towards Howley, who stopped it with his foot.

"Mark, hi. How are ya pal?" Howley said.

He shoved the chair back to Villicus. A front wheel slipped over the edge, allowing the metal leg to drag across the concrete, sending up a shower of sparks. Villicus caught him easily.

"This guy a friend of yours? Doesn't have a lot to say," Howley commented.

Villicus spun Hadley about and sent him flying along the

ledge back to Howley. Hadley did his best to scream past the frog, its legs flapping in the wind.

"He's pretty quiet...now," Villicus told him.

Howley shoved him back.

"Speak up, son!"

As the chair approached Villicus he neatly stepped up and out of the way. Hadley sailed right past him, then off the edge and out into space. Howley sauntered over to Villicus and the two vampires watched the chair spinning end over end until it hit a large neon sign on top of a shorter building across the street, advertising rocket fast internet services. The glass shattered, and sparks flew up in a dense shower, temporarily backlighting Hadley as he continued his descent to the street below.

The chair hit the ground hard, separating Hadley from his bindings. His body flopped across the pavement, then came to rest with one of his arms dangling down into a sewer. The chair spun across the intersection and was smashed to pieces by a truck carrying newspapers to local vendors who would open their little kiosks in just an hour or so.

"Whoops," Howley said, then continued, "So, tell me again why we did this? I mean, it was fun. Didn't you have fun?"

"Absolutely. Most fun I have had in centuries."

"Oh bad, very bad. You need better material. I'll get my writers right on that for you."

The two vampires sat down on the ledge, over thirty stories above the street, and watched the body on the ground. No one had seen it yet. It would be another couple of hours before anyone actually took notice. This was such an ignominious end for Mark Hadley.

A couple of rats crawled out of the sewer where his arm had fallen. They ran around him, then over him, then back into the sewer again. It was difficult to tell from their perch, so high up, but it did appear as if that arm was shaking slightly.

It appeared as if the rats were getting busy.

On top of the Delancey building, Howley and Villicus watched emergency vehicles arriving below to put out the fire caused by the exploding sign across the street. Hoses were moved about and tied into fire hydrants. Some firefighters with axes let themselves in the front door. Through a few windows near where the sign exploded, some bright orange and yellow flames shone through. Thick coils of black smoke found their way outside through minor defects in the casements.

A small explosion went off inside, punching a hole through the wall and sending huge chunks of glass, metal, wood and what pieces were left of the sign plummeting to the ground. Down below, firefighters and police scrambled about to avoid being crushed.

"Impressive! Seriously, hats off to you dude. You don't just kill someone, you burn an entire building down while you are doing it," Howley said.

"Dude?"

"Yeah, dude. Deal with it. Look where you are. Look when you are. You have to adapt better Villy, or you constantly risk being discovered."

"Villy?"

"Yes! What, you don't like that?"

"No."

Howley laughed and turned back to watching the human drama unfolding below them. News crews were arriving and fighting for the best spots to put up their cameras. The microwave towers on their vans went up, and in seconds, the story was transmitting.

The two vampires watched for a little longer, silently wondering when Hadley would be discovered. So far, no one had.

Howley turned to Villicus.

"So Villy, wanna tell me what this is about?"

He disregarded the casual, plebian pronunciation of his name. To him, it sounded vulgar, the way he would address a servant. He was though, dealing with Howley who was having a good time trying to rile him up, so he ignored it. Of any of the vampires he knew, Howley was the one he preferred to spend time with, mostly because he was so vulgar, and he always found a way to make him laugh. After a moment, he responded.

"Amanda."

"Amanda? What! A woman?"

"There's something about her. I think I need your help."

"For what?"

"I want her Howley. I want her..."

Looking down at Mark Hadley's remains splattered across the asphalt below, Villicus wondered how Amanda would react when she discovered that this ass, who had been making her life miserable, was no more. He hoped she would be so delighted. For a moment, he closed his eyes and imagined the enormous smile on her face that he put there, until Howley spoke up again and snapped him out of his reverie.

"You want to make her like us, don't you?" Howley continued.

"Yes."

"Are you fucking nuts? Have the same woman with you for eternity?"

Villicus lay back on the roof and covered his eyes with his forearm. His thoughts, usually streamlined and on target, were muddled and confused. What was happening to him? He tuned Howley out for a moment and let his thoughts run wild, just to see where they might go.

They did not seem to go anywhere, and things in his head were more jumbled than ever. Howley spoke to him, bringing him back into the moment.

"I think you need to get out of here for a while, think all of this over before you make an ass of yourself...Villy."

Villicus sat up, then shoved Howley off the top of the building. Sighing, he leaned forward and saw the cheeky vampire, just below him, perched effortlessly on a window ledge barely five inches wide.

News helicopters were showing up, circling the area, well above a police helicopter which was maneuvering about the buildings. The powerful spotlight, that Nightsun, was turned on and aimed at the building on fire, looking for more hotspots.

One of the news choppers stopped circling above the burning structure and flew over to the Delancey building. The pilot turned on a floodlight, illuminating Villicus sitting up on the edge of the building and Howley still perched just below him.

"Crap! Come on, we gotta go, *now!*" Howley shouted.

"Amanda?"

"Okay, fine, let's go get her. I'm with ya on this one, but we need to vacate the premises!"

"No, not like that."

"What do you mean?"

"I need to let her make her own decision."

"You are nuts. Why? If you want her, just take her. Hell, I'll do it for you. Happily! We could do this whole snuff film thing. It would be great! Make a few bucks while you get a girlfriend."

Howley climbed easily back up onto the rooftop next to Villicus. Together, the two of them walked towards the open doorway, ignoring the news chopper and the floodlight they now had shining on them. Near the opening, Villicus picked up the door he had shattered and threw it at the helicopter. The door, spinning like a giant disc, sliced into the base of the helicopter, ripping the camera and light system to shreds.

Pieces of metal and embers rained down on the roof and to the street below. Villicus could see the pilot and reporter on board staring in shock at what they had just witnessed, then quickly peeling off, looking for a safe place to land as they too began to ignite.

Villicus and Howley stepped towards the open doorway. The news chopper, now fully on fire, raced right by them, the faces of the terrified pilot and reporter framed by the windows while smoke billowed around them inside the cabin. They were headed to a nearby park, just two blocks away.

The two vampires completely ignored the drama racing right past them.

"Can you just tell me what the mystery is here with this woman?" Howley asked.

"If I knew that, I would tell you, but I don't."

Exasperated, Howley shook his head.

"I think I'll plan a little excursion for us. Some mandatory fun might be just what you need."

Villicus and Howley entered the smashed open doorway and disappeared inside. Across the street, up on top of a Bank of America building, Nikonar watched them from the shadows.

Chapter Twenty

A few hours later, just as the sun was peeking up along the eastern edge of Los Angeles, Amanda, somber and tired from the disappointing evening before, drove through the lightly filled streets. In just another hour or so, traffic would be a bitch, so she hurried along to get to the Delancey building. Her goal was to focus on work and avoid fixating on the events with Villicus the night before, although her presence was not required at the office that day, having been given some time off by her boss to rest after the events which occurred at Checkers. Amanda, though, was like a caged lion in her home and needed the order of her office and work to help calm her nerves.

As she made the final turn to the main entrance of the underground parking for the Delancey building, she saw yellow police tape, just a second too late, and drove partly under a section. Staring in amazement, she saw the entire street blocked off, including access to the main entrance. No one was around, and she sat there, her foot on the brake, staring at the tape and the parking structure beyond.

Lots of police were combing the area, and a small crowd of people, mostly homeless and bedraggled looking folks, gathered along the edges of the tape, straining to see what was going on. Police vehicles, their lights flashing, caused all of the street level windows in the area to light up with the sparkling candy colors and imbued a surreal feeling to the scene.

A sharp rapping sound on her window startled Amanda, and she whipped her head around to see a cop, tapping on the glass. Quickly, she rolled the window down.

"Oh my gosh, officer, what is going on?"

Polite, but clearly not wanting to enter into much of a conversation with her, he said, "I'm sorry ma'am, but you need to clear the area."

From the corner of her eye, Amanda saw movement near the front of her car, and turned to see another officer lifting the crime scene tape up where it had snagged on a section of the bumper of her car. Once it was free, he tapped her hood, gave a thumb's up sign then shooed her away.

"Oh no, you don't understand..." Amanda stammered.

Clearly losing some of his politeness and patience, the officer told her quickly and curtly, "Ma'am, you need to back out of here and vacate the area."

The other officer who had freed the tape from her car stood to one side, watching her carefully. She could see his hand resting on the butt of his gun.

Confused and unsure how exactly to proceed, Amanda continued, "But I work here."

She pointed at the blocked off entrance to the underground parking structure. Up ending her purse on the passenger seat, she frantically dug through everything there until she found her Delancey ID and showed it to them.

Both of the cops looked at the ID then turned to see where she was pointing. The one at her window shrugged, then said to her, "We can let people in the building. Your head of security is here, and he will clear everyone going inside. Is there somewhere else you can park?"

Amanda nodded, then backed the car out and headed around the block towards the back of the building where there was auxiliary parking. Through the side streets and narrow alleyways, the flashing lights from police vehicles sparkled, drawing everyone in the area to the scene. Whatever was going on here had her on full alert.

As she drove, very slowly, to the alley that led to the extra parking, she could see a cluster of people standing about near a sewer opening. Another group of officers were gathered near something draped under a white cloth on the asphalt and they were all staring intently at something on the ground.

The inevitable cavalcade of news crews were staking out areas nearby to broadcast their stories.

She wondered if another homeless person had been found in a nearby dumpster and shivered at the thought, but then quickly dismissed it.

The police had not been near any of the alleyways. They were right there on the street, staring at something on the ground. Maybe it was a bomb or something? A strange package perhaps left on the ground instead of a body? What in the hell was going on? She needed to get inside and find Blake as soon as possible. He would tell her.

Entering the rarely used back entrance to the underground parking, Amanda quickly exited her vehicle. Rushing towards the elevators, she saw Mark Hadley's car, parked in her boss's parking slot, with another cadre of police in and around it.

Oh my God, Amanda thought to herself and started to feel a swell of anger. "Mark, you ass, what did you do?"

Quickly exiting her vehicle, feeling more and more unsettled, partly from her hangover but mostly from the weirdness going on around her, she hustled towards the elevators. At the elevator banks, she saw another group of police gathered around. One of the doors was wedged open, surrounded by yellow police tape. Holding her ID in hand, she could not help but quietly walk up to peek at what they were looking at.

Standing there, near the open doors, she could hear a hideous version of *Copa Cabana* sputtering. Looking up at the speakers to see what might causing the nasty audio problems, she could see a shoe jammed into one of them.

What in the hell? She thought.

A police officer turned and saw her there, holding out her Delancey ID, and quickly ushered her into, of all things, the filthy shipping elevator, covered inside with dirty moving quilts. She did her best not to touch anything as she stepped inside. The officer, waving nicely to her, smiled as he pressed the button for the lobby. As the door closed, she realized too late, that there were not any lights on in the car.

Amanda quickly retrieved her phone and turned on the screen to give herself a little light to see by. Before long, the door opened, letting her out into the lobby of the office.

Near the front desk, she saw her boss, Gaines, talking in hushed tones to Delancey's head of security, Blake Hogan. Behind them, she also saw their cover girl receptionist, Jilly, crying quietly in her chair, her headset hanging askew from her head. Amanda rushed over to them, hating the loud tapping sound from her shoes announcing her approach.

Gaines and Hogan stopped their conversation and turned to face her.

"J.!" Amanda blurted out, then cringed at the booming sound of her voice as she watched Jilly's slender, perfectly formed shoulders shuddering with her sobs. "J.," she said more quietly, "What is going on here?"

Gaines faced her, and she could see him take a deep, controlled breath.

"Amanda. I...we have some bad news."

Shaking her head, still trying to take in everything, she stared at him, truly perplexed at what was going on.

Gaines continued, "Amanda, its Mark Hadley."

"Mark?" she asked, trying to hide the disgust in her voice. "What did he do?"

Gaines and Hogan both appeared a bit confused by her question. Then, Gaines reached out and held her by her shoulders.

"Amanda. Mark is dead." He said gently.

Stunned, Amanda pulled away from him and took a step back, blinking her eyes from disbelief.

"No! What...where? Here?"

She looked around and saw Jilly had stopped crying, her red eyes stained with mascara. Her headset looked almost comical hanging at such a silly angle from her head.

"No," Hogan interjected. "His body was found outside on the street."

Immediately, guilt crashed in on Amanda over her assumption that Hadley had done something stupid. The scene outside, all of the tape and the officers milling about, made sense now.

"What happened? How did he die?" she asked quietly.

"He fell to his death, the police think, from off of the roof," Gaines told her.

Jilly, calmer now, pulled the headset off and set it on the reception desk, starting to wipe the smeared mascara from her eyes with a tissue.

Looking back and forth between Gaines then Hogan, Amanda was trying to make sense of this.

"Are you kidding me? He jumped?"

"Not unless he tied himself to a chair before he did it," Hogan said quietly.

Jilly buried her face in the mascara-stained tissue and started to sob again.

An hour or so later, Amanda sat in a chair in the hallway near her office, feeling numb. Her fingers were wrapped tightly around a cup of coffee someone had thought to bring her. The liquid was hot. The cup should have been burning her fingers, but she barely felt it.

A detective had come and taken her statement. Clearly, she was considered a potential suspect. She was so out of it the night before, though, she really did not know what time Villicus had left her home. When she told the detective he had left probably around midnight or so, the look in his eyes and the rapid way he wrote his name down in his notes communicated to her that they would want to question him as well.

Amanda had wanted to shout out that Villicus had nothing to do with any of this but held her words. She knew if she blurted them out, even she would not believe them.

Had Villicus been involved in this?

Not wanting to believe, and even more so not wanting to contemplate the possibility, she pushed it from her mind.

The heat from her cup finally got to her, and she dropped it onto a nearby table, immediately sorry for the coffee that slopped onto the pretty rug. What she wanted was her morning surprise drink that Paul would bring to her. Looking about, and seeing his desk outside her door, she searched for his smiling face. Where was he?

"Paul?" she called out but did not get a response. "Paul?"

Amanda rose and walked briskly to his work area. Paul Peter's desk was as pristine as it always was. She looked over his desk, trying to see signs that he had been there this morning but did not spot anything. From across the hall, she saw Midge, another trader's assistant, and asked if she had seen Paul Peter that morning.

"No," Midge said, as she rifled through her purse, pulling out a set of car keys. The woman, in her late forties and usually quite stoic, appeared a bit nervous as everyone else skittered around the office. A few had already headed home, too rattled to get any work done. "Maybe he took a sick day."

"If that little toad is at home nursing a hangover..." she whispered under her breath.

Amanda, not convinced because he always texted and emailed her, turned and headed back to her chair in the hall. Plopping down, she slowly rolled over to the floor to ceiling windows and stared down at the scene below. From that angle, the crisscrossing yellow police tape resembled a huge kite shape. She could only hope that it might catch the wind and sail away.

The roof was still a few floors above her, and she could only imagine what a horror it had been for Hadley, falling such an enormous distance, tied to a chair no less. She shuddered to think of the amount of time he had on the way down, wrapped tightly in utter terror and panic. She winced, then turned with a start when she heard footsteps coming up behind her. J. Richmond Gaines, looking tired and haggard, stood there. He was trying to tell her something, and it was clear, he was having a very difficult time doing so.

What now? Amanda wondered. *What else?*

Chapter Twenty-One

Amanda sat, where she had sat all day, in a chair by the window inside her living room overlooking the city. She had watched the sun move across the city, the shadows lengthening and people scurrying about, doing whatever it was that took up their time.

Around her ankles, on the floor, sat several balled-up tissues. Her eyes were so red and inflamed from crying that she felt they would surely bleed if she shed another tear and wiped it away. But again, they fell down her face. She had known sadness in her time, but never felt so awash with sorrow, so utterly impaled by grief.

When Gaines had approached her earlier that morning, she was sure that he was there with more hideous news about the death of Mark Hadley. Out of respect for his position of authority in the company, she had risen from her chair and walked over to speak with him when he showed up. When he delivered the news to her that the body of Paul Peter had been found on the grounds of the aquarium, her knees actually buckled.

He managed to catch her before she hit the ground.

She was horrified at the news and at first failed to comprehend what Gaines was saying. All too aware that her body had failed her and she lay on the ground at his feet, slack jawed and nearly quivering, she tried to absorb the news of Paul Peter's death.

Blake Hogan had been immediately summoned, as Gaines, although a competent leader in his corporate kingdom, was helpless to Amanda's immediate condition. She was aware of Midge rushing in and kneeling down next to her, compassionate hands wrapping gently around her face and turning her gaze upward, trying to gauge whether or not Amanda had fainted or was merely incapacitated by the news.

Hogan thundered in, quickly gathering Amanda up into his arms and carrying her to a couch in the hallway. Amanda wished he had not, as others in the offices rushed out to see what this latest commotion was about. Shortly thereafter, she had managed to get into a sitting position but was unable to answer questions put to her. Dumbly she sat in morose silence.

All of it, everything that had happened in the past twenty-four hours, was too much. It was all too much to bear, and she shut down.

Those around her determined she was okay, just disabled by the news, and a driver was summoned who quickly spirited her home. Midge had accompanied them, driving Amanda's car, and helped her inside to the chair where she had remained all day.

Before she left, Midge put a box of tissues on a table by the chair along with a glass of orange juice, a small plate of cookies, and Amanda's phone. Sternly, but compassionately, Midge ordered her to call if she needed anything. Amanda finally raised her eyes to meet Midge's and nodded she would. There was only one call she had placed during the day, and that was to Villicus. He had not answered, so she left a short but calm message, telling him about the deaths that had intruded so rudely on the day. After she hung up, she sobbed so hard, her ribs actually ached.

Where was he? Did the police have him? Did he have something to do with Hadley's death?

Darkness crept up over her garden walls, and the city below, looking dirty and cramped in the sun, took on its nightly endless, jewel-like appearance. The magical transition from filth to fantasy that usually brought her so much joy did little to console her this evening. Her phone had rung a few times during the day; however, it was not him. Gaines had called, as had Hogan, and both times she was polite but kept the conversation very short, telling them both she was okay. They knew she was not but respected her need to be alone.

A knock at the door drew her up and onto her feet. Appalled by the collection of used tissues scattered at her feet, she bent to clean them up, then decided the effort was not worth it. Nothing felt worth it to her right now.

Amanda, in stocking feet, needed to stand on tiptoes to see through the tiny viewport of her front door. Backlit by the few rays of the recently set sun, Villicus stood outside the door, stock still, holding a single rose.

She let him into the hallway, her pain filling the small space. Villicus did not hand her the rose. Instead, he set it down on a small table near the door.

Turning to her, he asked, "What can I do?"

"I don't know," she whispered hoarsely, her voice sadly compromised from crying. "I don't have any friends. Paul was my friend. Now he's gone."

In an attempt to console her, he said, "Amanda, it is only death. There are things that are much worse."

Stunned by his words, Amanda quickly felt her sorrow replaced by red hot anger.

"What do you mean *it's only death*!" she snapped at him. "What the hell would you know about it?"

Villicus remained still, impassive, towering above her. Her outpouring did not seem to disturb him, although his brow furled slightly, indicating his confusion to her harsh words.

Amanda felt empty again and pushed herself against his chest, crying. Villicus looked down at her, watching her body convulse from the sobs. He tilted his head to one side for a moment, as if remembering something, then awkwardly wrapped his arms around her.

Amanda's heavy sobbing subsided, and she asked him, "Please stay with me, just for tonight?"

Villicus raised one hand and gently pulled up a few strands of her hair, letting them drift through his fingers.

"Yes, for you I will," he said.

Tears still rolled down her cheeks, and she looked so vulnerable, so pathetic. When he had said yes, she managed to take a deep breath and felt somewhat of a sense calm wash over her.

He rose to his feet, with her still in his arms, and carried her to the bedroom.

Villicus sat on her bed, fully clothed. Amanda, freshly bathed and wearing a pink nightgown, crawled up between his legs to snuggle against his chest. She felt more refreshed after having had a hot bath; however, the events of the day had taken their toll. She was exhausted.

His arms fell to his sides as she pushed up against him. Slowly, he wrapped his arms around her and lost himself in the subtle rhythm of her breathing. As before, having her pushed up against him so, his darker side began to emerge. Gently, he trailed his fingers down her back and watched her body relax, then writhe slightly under his touch.

Villicus felt his eyes transform into black tarns as he kneaded the muscles in her back, then reached down and cupped her bottom, pulling her closer into him. He could feel her breath quicken as she became aroused.

Curling himself tightly around her, he tried to feel the sensations she was experiencing. He wanted very much to sense the erotic arousal and response to touch that he himself could no longer feel. For as many humans as he had fed upon, his compassion for them was devoid; however, his desire to understand how his power affected them remained a fascination for him.

She did nothing to entice or encourage him and, in her dreamy state, let him make up his own mind. He reached down and gently trailed his fingers over her breasts. Her breathing became heavier, more labored, and her back arched dramatically.

Villicus reached up and laced his fingers through her hair, then pulled her head back hard, exposing her neck to his greedy mouth. His lips parted, allowing the points of his teeth to aim towards his target.

Amanda was gone now, thrashing in a sea of lust. Villicus widened his mouth and quickly tapped his teeth together, almost like a nervous tick, as he leaned down, ready to take her. Just as his lips brushed along the side of her neck, and he felt the pulse of her blood rushing just under the surface, a part of him screamed, "Stop".

Slightly panicked, he pulled quickly away from her, startled by his reaction. Where had that voice come from? What was happening to him?

Frustrated, Amanda snapped into the moment and became fully awake; however, he placed one large hand over Amanda's eyes, preventing her from seeing his transformed state, his terrifying blackened eyes and massive, tearing teeth. Briefly, she struggled against him, but Villicus held her tightly and moved his hand down between her legs, stroking her there until she again let herself go and succumbed to his touch.

Villicus kept his hand clamped firmly over her eyes as she climaxed. He held her, perplexed by what he had just experienced within himself. Her breath, made rapid and heavy by her arousal, slowly resumed to a steady rhythm. Villicus stayed with her through the night, holding her so and replaying that jolt of panic he had felt, trying to understand what was happening to him.

She had fallen asleep immediately after he had removed his hand from her eyes, and she stayed that way through the night.

Through her bedroom window, he caught sight of the first rosy rays of the dawn and departed, vampire quick, towards the front door. Amanda was still falling back onto the pillow as he made his exit.

The rose he left on the table for her was the only clue that he had been there.

Chapter Twenty-Two

Quietly, Detective Kim Barnstall worked at her desk. She had called up more information from the medical examiner and carefully compared notes from all of the related murders. As she came across interesting similarities, she messaged them to James, her partner, at the desk right across from her. There had to be a solid thread, and perhaps, the answer to finding that lay in the discrepancies between the killings, not so much the similarities.

She did not know yet but had confidence they would find it.

Across from her, with each note she shot over to him, James responded with a nod of his head or a quick grunt as he accessed similar files. Together, they worked like this, piecing bits of information together to find that arrow, that direction, which would lead them to whatever psycho was doing these bizarre, brutal, killings.

Both had agreed it was a serial killer, and probably just one; however, a recent victim found sitting in a chair in a nightclub indicated two. It was a frustrating game.

Their captain, Raul Mazurka, rail thin with premature silver hair, walked towards them. Kim saw his approach and hoped he was going to move past them to another group of detectives behind them; however, he stopped right at the juncture of hers and James' desks.

Kim turned a smiling face up to him and asked, "Can I help you Captain?"

He moved around to peer over her shoulder at the gruesome autopsy photos she had been studying.

"Anything new?"

"Still working it, you know how it is."

"Yup."

James paused what he was doing and looked up at the two of them.

"Here," the Captain continued. "This just arrived. I think it belongs to the two of you."

He handed her a note, written on exquisite cream-colored paper. The handwriting was like a work of art, each word and letter placed exactly so on the envelope. It was addressed to the "Detectives in charge".

"Wow," Kim said, as she pulled on some latex gloves then proceeded to remove the note from inside. "What makes you think this is for us? I don't really feel in charge of anything at the moment."

James rose and rolled his chair around to sit next to her.

"Well, I read it already," the Captain explained to her. "Keep going."

"Did you get it processed yet?" she asked.

"No, so after you are done, you'll need to process it. I doubt there are any prints, but with the arrogance written in there, you never know."

"Okay."

Kim pulled the note out and carefully opened it. The writing inside was again phenomenal. She had never seen anything so precise and beautiful. It looked like writing she had seen in museums from the middle ages of illuminated manuscripts. It was just missing the cherubs, decorated initials and elaborate borders to enhance the writing.

"Wow," she whispered.

"Wow is right," James said as he looked over her shoulder. "Looks like it might have been written with a quill pen or something."

"Hmmm, maybe," Kim mused. "CSI can tell us more. Sure as hell was quite a production."

Together, they read the note while their Captain looked on.

My dear police.

Undoubtedly, you are really scratching your heads over the recent series of killings in this, our beautiful City of Angels. Might I suggest you keep tabs on a certain movie producer named Howley Bennett. Casting your eye in that direction might turn up more than you bargained for.

"It's not signed," Kim noted.

"But he refers to Los Angeles as 'our beautiful city'. He must live here. Who is this Bennett guy?" James asked.

"A movie producer, like the letter says. Makes cheesy action films and some slasher pictures," the Captain said.

"Does he have a sheet?" James asked.

"Not so much as a parking ticket."

"Doesn't sound like the kind of guy we're looking for," Kim stated, bringing the note up close to her face.

"Neither did Ted Bundy. Put a tail on 'im."

"You got it," James said as he rose and pushed his chair back to his desk, then started to type information into his computer.

"At that last crime scene," the Captain asked Kim, "you found a handkerchief?"

"Yes, linen, hand-hemmed, fairly expensive but not that unusual. It was saturated with the victim's blood."

"Did that turn up anything?"

"No, nothing yet."

He sighed heavily, then said to her, "Keep at it, Kim. Keep working it. You'll find him."

"Or it," she thought, as she glanced back over at her computer monitor with the lurid images of torn throats from the victims splashed across her screen.

Chapter Twenty-Three

A huge, red, vintage 1953 Cadillac Eldorado glided up to the entrance of Villicus's building. The doorman stuck his head inside the passenger window, nodded, then headed inside. A few moments later, Villicus stepped out into the night and smiled broadly when he saw the behemoth vehicle in front of him.

The top slowly peeled back and a smiling Howley, wearing dark shades, waved at him. Villicus laughed and then waited until the top was all the way down before he stepped into the boat of a car.

"Nice," he said. "I like this."

"I thought you might."

"So, this mandatory fun you spoke of. Where are we headed to engage in that?"

"Oh, you'll love it. Trust me."

"But I don't, trust you that is, so tell me now."

Howley burst out laughing, then put the car in gear and headed down towards the Avenue of the Stars. The vintage vehicle, beautifully maintained, slipped into traffic and cruised towards the entrance to the freeway.

"Fine, you are such a pain in the ass, you know that? South of the border, mi amigo! Okay?"

"Amigo?"

"It's Spanish."

"Is it?"

"Yeah. Don't worry. You don't need to speak the language there, though."

"As if that really makes a difference."

Howley laughed again as he motored the car into traffic. The massive size and pristine condition of the vehicle caused the other drivers to slow down to take a look. He took his time maneuvering the car into the lane he wanted, even waving at a few of the other drivers who waved back or nodded in his direction, indicating their respect and admiration for his ride.

They headed across town, then onto the 405 South. An unmarked police car had slipped into the traffic and cautiously zigzagged behind them, keeping a few cars between them and the Caddy.

At the crossing into Tijuana, the police car pulled off to one side and parked, staying on the American side.

The two vampires drove into Tijuana, which was lit up like a party float. Loud, upbeat music filled the air, and the streets were jam packed with people partying. Villicus had turned around in the seat and was on his knees, looking up and around at everything, completely fascinated by all the raucous partying going on around them.

"What is this?" Villicus asked, amazed at all of the people and partying.

"The Day of the Dead, my friend."

Villicus was sure he was having fun with him and turned around again, sliding down into the seat. Carefully he studied Howley, who drove the Caddy into a small building and then turned the car off.

"You joke?"

"Nope! This is just the ticket for you. It's a big deal down here."

They exited the car, then closed up the building, locking the Caddy safely inside.

The two set off on foot, wading through the thick crowds of people while Howley explained the history of the festival to Villicus. The city was decked out with skeletons and brightly colored decorations. Throngs of party goers, many dressed as skeletons, danced in the streets. Howley walked Villicus past a small, local graveyard and pointed out several families who were camped out for the night next to the graves of loved ones, there to honor the spirits of those who had passed.

Villicus found the whole concept particularly fascinating. His experience with death had been primarily a personal one, where he himself ripped a life away and then simply discarded the body without any fanfare—no parties or dancing skeletons were ever involved. He was also familiar with the dreary funerals, many of which he had listened to for centuries buried deep beneath that morbid cathedral in Germany. Surrounded by such revelry focused on death was indeed a magnificent change of pace.

Howley had been right. He was not going to admit it yet, but he was actually enjoying himself.

Heading towards the outskirts of the town in an older section of the city, the two vampires shopped for victims in some of the local cantinas. As a rule, they tended to steer clear of those who were too inebriated. Too much alcohol spoiled the taste of the blood.

At a small cantina filled with music and lots of drunk partiers, near a truck repair shop and a small taqueria, they noticed some girls chatting outside, sipping wine and comparing what appeared to be new shoes they were wearing.

Howley and Villicus enticed them into a nearby alley, and both vampires gorged on the women, then dumped their bodies into an open drain where they sank out of sight.

As the evening wore on, the partying in the town toned down slightly; however, the music and dancing in the streets still hit some pretty impressive decibels. To get away from the noise but still enjoy the city, Howley and Villicus found themselves perched on top of an old mission-style church not far from the cantina where they had feasted on the young women. Howley was leaning comfortably up against the old cross, while Villicus had nestled down nearby in a small group of carved stone gargoyles.

"Do you still want her?" Howley asked.

"Yes."

"What difference does it make then if the decision is hers or not? Why not just take her?"

Howley paused for a moment and pointed out some fireworks in a nearby graveyard. The two of them watched the display, the amazing colors splashing against their pale faces.

"Do you love her?" Howley asked.

"Love her? I don't know what that is…"

Howley could not believe what he was hearing. Villicus, one of the most powerful vampires he had ever met, was actually stammering.

"Maybe you do. You know, each one of us retains a tiny bit of what we were when we were still human. An essence remains."

"Do you really think so?"

"Why not?"

He really was not sure how old Howley was but was certain that was not his name. He wanted to ask several times why he made it up but decided that he did not really care. This vampire had his reasons and if he wanted Villicus to know, he would have told him by now.

Howley was older than him, he was sure of that, but again, he did not know by how much and never asked. Right now though, while he was sharing information about their kind that Villicus did not know, he could not help but wonder how Howley knew such things.

"Partner, what in the hell is rolling around in that head of yours?" Howley asked.

"How do you know these things?"

Howley bellowed such a loud laugh that a woman down on the street below could hear him. Both vampires watched with great amusement as a group of people looked all around, trying to figure out where the noise had come from.

"We pick up things over the years. Some we were told about by our makers, other things from experience, that's all."

Villicus decided to let that part of their conversation go. There would be other times to discuss Howley's origins. Right now, he was actually more intrigued by what Howley believed he retained from his human self.

"What about you? What do you retain?"

"Promise not to laugh?"

Villicus let out a loud guffaw and slapped his knee. Apologizing, he urged Howley to continue. "Okay, I promise."

"I can still dream. Do you dream, Villicus?"

"No."

"When I rest, I can still see dreams, about people and places I've seen. I can see the sun and taste food and Merlot, cigarettes and... pussy."

Howley barked out a loud laugh again and sighed remorsefully.

Done below, a couple of people heard him this time. They looked around, startled, trying to figure out where this noise came from. One of them, crossed themselves and ran.

"Is that a good thing?"

"What do you mean?"

"What's the use of dreaming if you can't have those things when you are awake?"

Howley shrugged his shoulders, then continued.

"Bale had you bricked up under that church for a long time."

"Six hundred years."

"How the hell did you survive?"

"I don't know, really. I prayed for death many times."

"You prayed? Do you think God still listens to us?"

"I do not know. I prayed for death, instead I was released. I'm here now, with you. I know I want Amanda to be with me. Those things are all that I know."

"And Bale? What about Bale and that crazy Russian? Those are the jokers that buried you away. They could do it again you know. What do you think about those two?"

"Oh Nikonar, he can go his own way. I don't think he has the sense to survive on his own or attempt to come after me again. But Bale, he should be obliterated."

"You plan on destroying him?"

"I'm not done playing with him yet. He deserves to suffer for what he did to me. I don't know which he loves more, money or killing..."

"Yeah, that's a tossup. Be careful of him, Villicus. The world is a big place. Why don't you leave him alone? Head to New York maybe or Singapore..."

"The world surely is not big enough, as long as I know he is in it. He deserves to perish, but first, I will topple that incredible empire of his and destroy the power he craves so much."

"It's just a game."

Villicus rose and walked towards Howley, kicking the small gargoyles at his feet into dust.

"And I like that game! Its domination and manipulation. It's what drives the herds."

He pointed to the crowds below, weaving through the colorful streets where people danced and bobbed, weaved and staggered drunkenly past and into each other. Villicus mimicked the dancing and staggering movements as he pirouetted around the rooftop, kicking more statuary to bits.

"Besides, he isn't as smart as you say. Look at all the bodies he has left lying around these past weeks."

"Don't underestimate him."

"Why?"

"He does that every century or so, just to get everyone in a twist. Then he stops, and one of us always pays the price. Never him, mind you. It's just another game he plays. Come on, let's get going. Your lady awaits in far off LA."

They dropped down easily the eighty feet or so to the ground and moved past families spending the night near the graves of their loved ones. The people there stared in shock at these two beings who should surely have died from such a fall.

A few of the women crossed themselves and spit on the ground where the two vampires had walked past them.

The two continued laughing and chatting as they moved effortlessly through the thick crowd of partiers. Along the Avenida Revolucion, Howley stopped at one of the many street vendors and bought a huge black sombrero covered in gold and silver ornaments. To set the look off, he also bought a serape and a small face mask, that of a white skeleton, which covered just the top part of his face. After he put the mask on, Howley allowed his fangs to protrude. They went well with his costume.

For Villicus, he bought a fake gun in a holster and a huge moustache which he pushed onto the vampire's face. The moustache stuck where he placed it, although slightly askew. Thus attired, the two vampires continued their leisurely stroll through the herd, back to Howley's Caddy.

The huge, red chariot spirited them back to the border where their tail picked them up again at the crossing. The unmarked police vehicle, staying a few cars back, trailed them back into Los Angeles.

Curled tightly into a ball, Amanda slept fitfully as if ghosts, twisted shadows and monsters invaded her dreams, turning them into nightmares. A shadowy figure made its way across her bedroom towards her—soundless, large and imposing.

A thin thread of light made its way into her room from the moon outside, which hung low and fat over the Hollywood Hills. This late in the year, the evenings were much cooler, allowing thin layers of fog to gather close to the ground, enveloping her house in its cool embrace.

The figure kneeled on her bed and stopped, appearing to study her in her troubled sleep, then instantly was lying beside her. Amanda, unaware of the intruder, continued sleeping, her fingers gripping then releasing the top of the covers pulled up tightly under her chin.

Nikonar was with her, his frame so large next to her tiny, curled body that his feet hung off the end of the bed. Gently, just hovering above her body, he traced the contours of her curves with his fingers and leaned in close to her face so he could whisper to her.

"Hello, my sweet."

She stirred briefly and her eyes fluttered. Nikonar remained so still he truly did appear dead. After a moment, he gently placed his hand on her shoulder and whispered to her again.

"Amanda…so beautiful."

She stirred slightly but gave no indication of waking up. Nikonar trailed his fingers across her until he touched the diamond that Villicus had given to her. He had no way of knowing that it had been a gift from him, but somehow, he knew it and resisted the temptation to rip it right off her. He dropped it and continued to trail his fingers across her neck then down her back.

She writhed slightly under his touch. He smiled broadly, revealing thick fangs. He ran his tongue around his fangs as he gently probed her body, highly amused at her reaction to his presence, to his power.

Again, he leaned in to whisper to her.

"Villicus is going to kill you, Amanda."

Her brow furled, and she appeared upset and confused.

"He's a killer, Amanda. Remember that...he'll always be a killer."

With that last phrase he had so delicately whispered to her, Nikonar leaned in and licked the side of her face.

Amanda woke suddenly. Startled, she turned on a light and looked around the room. No one else was with her.

She shook her head, somewhat amused at having come awake from a bad dream, and reached out to turn the light off. The slight movement of her body caused a brief circulation of air over her skin. Feeling the coolness on the side of her face, she reached up with her fingers and was surprised to find that her cheek was wet.

Villicus exited Howley's ride, still wearing the moustache and gun, then headed into his building. Howley had removed his mask but was still wearing his huge sombrero and serape as he headed out, ready to go home after his night south of the border with Villicus. Across the street, the unmarked police car pulled over and waited at a discreet distance for him to glide the massive car back onto the pre-dawn street, completely empty this early in the morning. He had already turned onto Santa Monica Boulevard before the car moved out to follow him.

Inside, Villicus walked slowly and elegantly across the lobby, as was his custom, and ignored the startled look of the night concierge. However, there were often some fairly odd people costumed in all manner of outfits coming and going from the building, so the clerk quickly regained his composure and went back to his crossword puzzle.

Once Villicus arrived in his home at the top of this little world, he headed out to his rooftop aerie and stepped up on the ledge, his toes hanging precariously over the edge. He gazed up towards the Hollywood Hills, trying to imagine Amanda, sleeping sweetly in her bed with that pink nightgown on.

The wind tugged at his moustache, so he finally pulled it

off, letting it flutter off over the city. The gun and gun belt he removed but carried them back inside as a hint of dawn began to appear in the east.

Villicus entered his office, tossing the toy gun to one side, and turned on his computer. He used it only for email and had not learned how to do much else with it yet. The desktop image, though, was one he had figured out how to do while still in Germany. The picture that fluttered to life and greeted him was one showing several kittens sitting in a wicker basket. A ball of fluffy, pink yarn had been partially unwound, letting strands hang down from their ears. It was too adorable. The photographer had done a good job. All of the kitties were looking straight into the camera.

He liked their sweet little faces.

Calling up his email service, Villicus quickly prepared and then sent a note.

My dear Amanda. Please liquidate all shares of Radikale. I will call you soon — Villicus.

He tapped the send button, saw with satisfaction that the email appeared to have made its way through the cosmos to her, and then powered the machine down.

Villicus made his way to what served as his bedroom. He had had the room specially built in the center of the condo. There were no windows. The walls, floor and ceiling were actually a metal cage, not unlike a panic room, that was covered in drywall and painted a somber clay green color. He liked the soothing feel that color gave to him.

Once inside, he closed the door, which could only be opened from the inside with a submarine hatch. As soon as he sealed it and spun the wheel, an alarm system clicked on. Villicus had gone to great pains to ensure his privacy and safety. After all, he was now residing in the same city with the vampires who had imprisoned him once before, and Villicus was not going to allow that to happen again.

He was not terribly concerned about Nikonar, even though that bastard Russian had double-crossed him before. Villicus was more concerned about Bale. He knew that bastard was seriously different. He was a vampire, yet not. There was a power to Bale that Villicus somehow knew he was not completely aware of. This did concern him, and more than once, he thought about abandoning his plan to destroy Bale by destroying his lucrative empire, but the memories he had of being thrown away by him, locked away for centuries, fired up his burning hate again.

After double checking the alarm, he headed over to a small bed that occupied the middle of the room, covered only with a white, fitted sheet.

Villicus lay down and stared up towards the ceiling. Above him, mounted on an elaborate metal grid, were dozens of monitors, all turned on, revealing different live feeds to him from around the world. Next to the bed was a simple flywheel with a chain running around it. Villicus reached out, turned the wheel, and watched the display of monitors change. Some rotated up towards the ceiling, while others changed places with different monitors that had been further out to the side. The effect as they moved was not unlike a Calder sculpture rotating slowly in the wind.

He liked having the toy-like gizmo to shift them around by hand. He settled on a grouping above him that showed moonrise over Bali, the approaching dawn over Los Angeles, and a satellite view of the Pacific Ocean that showed jewel-like clusters all along the water's edge where massive cities existed, cities he would like to visit one day…with her.

There was no audio, just the streaming video. The majority of the other monitors had camera setups that automatically tracked the movement of the sun, and he was treated to images of bright daylight, sunrise and sunset from all about the globe.

Laying perfectly still, his gaze locked on the live feed showing the eastern border of Los Angeles. Just as the edge of the sun peeked up above the horizon, where his position on the planet was at this time, Villicus's eyes snapped shut, and he was at rest until the sun disappeared in the west.

Chapter Twenty-Four

Amanda had returned to Delancey, the only place where she could truly feel at ease, working and keeping herself busy. She hurried down the hall to her office, averting her eyes from Paul Peter's desk. Quickly, she entered through her door, then turned and looked back at his desk. Someone had already removed his personal things, and only a blotter and the phone remained. It was as if Paul Peter had never existed at all.

Feeling a surge of emotion, she turned and dashed inside, quickly shutting the door behind her. She needed to close the world out for now and just focus on work.

The police had been through every square inch of her office, and they, along with Blake Hogan, had piled up much of the items Mark Hadley had smashed onto a large canvas drop laying on the floor. She assumed they were going to let her go through what was left there, but after a quick scan, there was not anything she wanted back, especially not after Mark had his hands all over them.

She noticed right away that her computer had been replaced and was delighted to see it was a very new, very fast model. Firing it up and seeing that the password still worked, she quickly scanned the many emails and saw one from Villicus. Opening it, she pursed her lips in anger, then muttered, "Oh God. What the hell is he doing...?"

Before she could review his request or check any other emails, there was a light tapping at her door.

"Come in," she called out.

Gaines walked slowly and awkwardly into her office.

"Hi J." she said.

"Hiya, Amanda. Feeling better this morning?"

As he approached her desk, Amanda quickly turned a screen saver on so he could not see her email from Villicus.

"I'm hanging in there."

Gaines sat down across from her. Amanda winced slightly, remembering all the mornings Paul Peter sat across from her, helping her get the day started. It was not the same with her boss being there.

"That's good. I'm glad to hear it," he said, still keeping his tone light with her. "A lot has been happening around here this week. Some of the board members and myself have been trying to sort out what to do…what with Mark Hadley's death and all."

"And all?"

Gaines leaned forward, looking a bit embarrassed.

"You've been with us…how long now?"

"Four years," Amanda told him.

"Right. Mark had been with us for nine."

"And?"

"Well…he had been monitoring some of your accounts for us."

"What?!" she snapped at him.

"Amanda, that's how it is…"

"Don't fuck with me! Not now, J.!"

"Fine. Fine. Just relax. The thing is, the night Mark died, there was a partial transmission to our main frame from him, and it showed, well, it showed some irregularities in your accounts."

"Oh, please! You saw him that night at the party! You know what he was doing."

"Yup. You're right. You're right. Not everything can be accounted for that night, but we still have this information in our files. The police are going to want to look at those files… Amanda…"

"Oh, for God's sake! Think J.! Just think for a moment. Who do you think hacked us, huh? Who wanted more than anyone to walk over everyone to get where he wanted and what he wanted. Huh J.?"

"Look, Amanda. All we have is the evidence in front of us

right now. There is no proof he hacked the company he was working for. Mark met with me several times over the past year or so, and he told me he was suspicious of what you were doing, especially the large cash dealings you had going these past few months."

"Uh huh."

"We think it would be a good idea if you would take a few days off."

"We? We...okay, whatever."

"Just be patient with us until all this gets sorted out. Let your other clients know you will be out of the office for a few days and close up shop here right now. OK?"

"Right. Consider me gone."

She waved at him politely as he rose and left quickly. As soon as her door closed, she authorized the massive sale that Villicus had requested she do.

Amanda turned on her TV to watch the daily business report and kept an eye on the index out of New York. The numbers were already being affected by the huge sale she pushed through. Quickly, she pulled open the drawers of her desk and started to grab up personal items.

Pulling out the file with all of the notes from Villicus she saw the card with the kitten on it and smiled, thinking about Paul Peter's reaction to it. Continuing to stow all the notes and a few other items in her briefcase, she listened to the report on TV.

"...a steady climb along the patterned index, matching volumes from the past three days for heavy industry, crude and sweet oil," a reporter droned on, "Margins for the shipping industry and foreign investors tallying sales abroad, indicate that profits are well within sight for the three big companies, Darkin, Bolley and QRB Enterprises."

The reporter continued, and Amanda looked up to see graphics flying by on the TV, showing the stock market.

"A huge sale of stock in Radikale Holding Company, a Los Angeles-based firm, has apparently prompted a declaration for Chapter Eleven. An enormous stock sale, following another huge sale of stock in its sister company, Schwermut, a few days ago seems to have crumbled the foundation for both companies.

In related news, trading on the Japanese market is down due to this offering…"

Amanda sighed deeply, then sat back in her chair. It was done. Whatever bridges she had left at Delancey were now fully engulfed in flames.

Her door burst open, and an angry Gaines stormed in. Blake Hogan stood in the doorway, his hands on the frames, blocking the exit.

"What did you think you were doing?" Gaines shouted at her.

"Following the wishes of my client," Amanda said quietly.

"Do you realize how bad this makes us look? *Do you!*"

"Yes, and I'm sorry."

"You're fired!" Gaines told her, then turned to exit the office, snapping out an order to Hogan as he brushed past him. "Make sure she leaves today. *Now!*"

Across town, in his darkened office, Bale watched the same broadcast, furious, as the numbers dropped. His companies were dying.

His phone rang again, probably panicked officers from his companies. The dreary humans he kept on board to run things for him were watching their world collapse. He reached out without looking and picked the phone up, effortlessly squeezing it into a small ball of metal and glass before tossing it in the corner.

The ringing stopped.

His computer announced to him, "You have one hundred twenty-six emails, all marked urgent."

"Oh, oh, oh, this is nothing more than an inconvenience to me, Villicus," Bale hissed in the dark. "I do, though, believe it is time for a little retribution."

Amanda had left Delancey with Hogan trailing behind her, looking apologetic but firm. He carried a box with a few more items that belonged to her, the things that Mark Hadley had not destroyed. Together, they rode down a back freight elevator, and he walked her to her car.

After she unlocked it, he reached down and held the door for her. Without a word between the two, she got in and drove away.

Upon arriving at her house, she spent the day cleaning as she never had before and refused to turn the TV on or answer the phone or any emails. She felt like she was floating in a void and did not know what was going to happen for her next.

As the sun set on the wasted and empty day, Amanda's phone rang again. This time, though, she answered it.

"Amanda, I need to see you."

It was Villicus.

Chapter Twenty-Five

Howley's home was not far from his offices in West Hollywood. He preferred to be down in the city, in the thick of things, and loved to walk through the city streets in the evening to watch the tourists and the locals dining and chatting at open air restaurants along Santa Monica Blvd.

The sun had just set, but he was still resting, caught in the throes of a dream. In his dream, he was seated at a café on the banks of the river Seine in Paris. He was dressed in a bright, white suit and cool sunglasses. Golden rays of sunlight streamed through the trees and the tall buildings that crowded close to the river. Sitting at the table with him were several beautiful women who were dressed in different attire from the many ages he had existed in. Some of them had been his victims. They sat there, chatting and giggling with the other women, their throats ragged and bloody open wounds.

As they chatted with each other in their own languages—French, Spanish, German, Dutch and English—one by one, they started to float up into the air and sail away over the river. Howley sang "Lucy in the Sky with Diamonds" as he floated up after them.

His eyes snapped open, and he sat up, smiling. His dreams always made him smile. He was never able to understand them but did not care. He just loved the colors and sunlight, the sensations they brought to him.

His room was completely dark, no windows, and he clapped his hands, turning on some lights. The furniture was big and overstuffed, covered in plum and red velvet cloth. The rugs, thick and sumptuous piles, were also various shades of red and plum. He stood and exited the room, moving about his house, to turn on lights and all of his toys like TVs, stereo and computers, all running at the same time. Before long, his home, instead of being as quiet as a tomb, sounded like a cheap cantina.

Outside, two detectives had been staked out to watch him.

"Huh," one of them said, as he sipped cold coffee, "I guess the bastard is at home."

The other detective, on the far side of the car, scrunched down and looked through the windshield.

"Yeah, you're right. I didn't think anyone was in there either."

They watched as Howley left his house, jumped into his blood-red Caddy and drove off, headed towards the hills. A few moments later, the detectives followed at a distance, unaware of Bale and Nikonar following them in Bale's massive Mercedes.

This parade of cars trickled its way up into the windy side streets of the Hollywood Hills where Howley drove his car up onto the lawn in front of a house that had a huge and noisy party going on. He jumped out and headed inside, leaving his car parked on top of some azalea bushes. The detectives pulled up across the street and sat in wait, while Nikonar and Bale watched and waited as well in the distance.

Chapter Twenty-Six

Amanda entered Villicus's building and headed to the elevator, where she used a call box to ring his penthouse.

"Yes?"

His disembodied voice drifted through the com box, sounding hollow and forlorn.

Perfect, she thought, *he sounds like how I feel.*

"It's Amanda," she said.

The elevator doors parted for her and she entered.

From up in his aerie, Villicus watched her on one of his many security monitors. He saw her stare blankly at the floor of the elevator during the short, swift ride to the top. When the elevator arrived, he activated the locks for the foyer doors. He timed it all so she would see them swinging open into this foyer, and then the next set would swing open into his home.

Amanda exited, as if on cue, passing through the main doors into his penthouse. Entering the living room of his condo, she looked around, stunned at how much he had done with the place. It was surreal, with the massive sun sculpture on the ceiling glowing brightly and dozens of toys and hi-tech gizmos displayed, most of them turned on and running.

The small toy that she had given to him sat on a pedestal with its own spotlight.

A door on the far side of the room opened, and Villicus walked out towards her.

"So, how was your day?" she asked him.

"Restful. And yours?"

"Well, let's see. I lost my job! I'm being investigated by the

SEC for your accounts, I'm sure, and I think the police want to speak with me regarding Mark Hadley's death."

Villicus watched her quietly, his hands clasped in front. Amanda sighed heavily and walked past him to look out the windows.

"I just love this view you have. The city looks so beautiful at night, don't you think?"

Villicus walked up behind her.

"Do you like it?" he asked.

"Yes."

"Do you like it better at night?"

"Harder to see the flaws."

Amanda spun around to face him.

"Tell me the truth and don't lie to me! Have you been fucking with me?"

Villicus was truly puzzled by her question and tilted his head to one side, observing her coolly. Amanda stepped forcefully towards him and he took a step backwards.

"Answer me and don't lie! You've been using me, haven't you? Some sort of sick, demented game you've been playing. Haven't you?"

"Yes."

Amanda was stunned by his honesty and stared slack jawed at him. He stepped forward and took her by the hand.

"Come with me," he said.

He pulled her into the small elevator that rode them both up to the catwalk, and together they walked out onto the rooftop. Holding her hand tightly but gently, he led her to the edge of the roof and stepped up.

"No! Villicus, please stop. I can't...I can't do that."

He released her and sat down on the edge, his legs dangling over the side. Smiling, he turned to look back at her and held his hand out. Bit by bit, inching closer, she grabbed hold of his hand. Villicus held onto her tightly as she gingerly, and very carefully, sat down next to him.

Her breathing came in huge, ragged gulps. One of her shoes slipped off. Amanda leaned forward to see it tumble downwards and nearly slipped in the process, but Villicus still held her hand. She nearly fainted from fear.

"I won't let you fall," Villicus told her.

Up in the hills, the two detectives who had been tailing Howley were getting tired and frustrated from watching and waiting.

"He's probably in there getting his knob polished."

"Wish I was. Hey! Don't look at me that way."

The two laughed, then one stopped and elbowed the other.

"Look!"

They watched as Howley walked out of the house with a girl. She looked drunk and fell; however, Howley picked her up effortlessly and tossed her like a rag doll into the front seat of his car from nearly twenty feet away.

"Holy Christ, did you see that!?"

"Well, I'll be damned. Yeah! Let's roll on this."

The detective in the passenger seat got on the radio and let his superiors know what they had seen. They advised them that they were going to continue the tail and would intervene if they felt the girl was in danger.

Howley drove down and off the lawn, ripping out flowers and a hedge along the way. He bounced the Caddy down over the curb, his headlights raking over the police car. The two detectives ducked until his beams swept past him, then they started their car up and headed after him with Nikonar and Bale not far behind, travelling with their headlights off. Bale was driving and both he and Nikonar could see just fine without them.

The Caddy proceeded up the windy road until it intersected with Mulholland Drive, where Howley took a sharp turn to the right. He sped along the road at breakneck speed, the huge car barely hugging the sharp turns. He turned into a short drive at the entrance to one of the lookout points and put the car in park. As he exited the vehicle, Howley had the top come back up on the car, and he stepped out towards the gate where he easily snapped the lock and chain off with one hand.

After the gate swung open, he drove the Caddy into the small lot and secured the roof that had finally come all the way back up. The huge Hollywood sign glittered on the hill just up behind them.

The detectives pulled into the short drive at the gate, their headlights off.

"Call for backup!"

"Right."

"Do it now."

The detective driving the car inched in closer behind the Caddy that was rocking back and forth.

"Awesome!" one of them said. "Look, he's just doin' her."

"Yeah, maybe so. Let's just make sure."

The two exited their vehicle quietly and, with guns drawn, moved up on either side of the rocking, red car. One motioned that on three they would open the doors and then mouthed the countdown. On one, they snatched the doors open and were stunned to see Howley, his face a horror show of smeared blood and small bits of tissue hanging from his teeth. Snarling and growling, he looked up from the ripped throat of the girl, and his black gaze caused the detectives to stumble backwards, horrified at what they were seeing.

Howley picked up the body of the girl and threw her out the door, knocking one of the detectives down. He jumped out, terrifyingly fast, and grabbed the other detective. He lifted him up and off his feet, then sent him airborne down the hill. The detective landed in some shrubs nearly twenty feet down.

The other detective scrambled to get out from under the body of the dead girl and raced back to the car to get to the radio.

"We need backup now. *Now!* At Vista Point! *Now!*"

He grabbed the shotgun they kept locked down in the front seat, turned, and leveled it towards Howley's car.

He looked up in terror, seeing Howley's huge Caddy rocketing towards him. The detective jumped out of the way just as the bigger red car spun the smaller Cavalier around in the direction that they had arrived from. The officer ran into the street after Howley's car and fired the gun. Some sparks flew from the back where shot met metal; however, he was too late to slow the vampire down.

Howley sped back up the hill, unaware of Nikonar and Bale watching him quietly from the dark in a small grove of Eucalyptus trees off the side of the road. Their heads turned in unison as they watched the Caddy rip by them. They both burst out laughing.

"Ah yes, this is turning out to be quite the night," Bale laughed.

"More festivities in store?"

"Hmmmm, our work here is done, as they say. Time to head home and catch the news."

Just then, several police cars raced up Mulholland Drive after Howley. Nikonar and Bale laughed heartily again and as soon as the coast was clear, motored slowly onto Mulholland and turned towards Bale's palatial estate.

Miles up the road, Howley shut the lights off on his car and cranked up the music as he raced over eighty miles per hour through the twisty streets of the Hollywood Hills. His massive car bashed and dented dozens of cars jammed along the sides of the street. Side view mirrors, fenders and a couple of motorcycles were sent flying into front yards.

When he reached his street, he roared up the road, barely missing a small group of coyotes crossing. They leaped out of the way and disappeared into the rose garden of a cute little Cape Cod house perched on a miniscule corner lot. Howley glanced in the rear-view mirror but did not see anyone pursuing him.

He reached his drive and raced up it, slamming the brakes on the car, but the weight of the Caddy was a lot to slow down. He bashed into the side of his own house, taking out an entire side. Sparks flew from electrical wires being torn from the wall and reflected in hundreds of tiny surfaces from the shattered windows.

The car finally stopped and Howley, desperate to find refuge in his safe room, knowing nothing short of a small nuclear bomb could break into it, jumped from his car. Just as his feet hit the intricately patterned stones that made up his driveway, a light brighter than any sun he had sat under in his dreams hit him full force.

The roar of the police helicopter above his home was near deafening, its night sunlight trained squarely on him. Howley, his eyes still blackened and face twisted from the true evil that resided in him, leapt forward and was confronted by several police officers streaming from around both sides of his ruined home. He rushed forward, then seeing how many there were, decided on a different tactic.

He turned and lunged back into his Caddy, threw it into gear, and took off into the predawn darkness. He would find no refuge in his own home.

Amanda, a bit more at ease, sat quietly next to Villicus, waggling her feet still dangling over the edge, with one shoe off and one shoe on. Villicus held her hand tightly but not crushing her. She felt safe with him and did not even contemplate the lunacy of sitting on the edge of a twenty-two-story building, with nothing between her and the ground but air.

She turned her head slightly and caught the slightest blush of dawn beginning to steal its way across Los Angeles. Villicus rose, pulling Amanda up with him.

"Where are you going?" she asked.

"Back inside. Come with me, now."

"No, please. Stay and watch the sunrise with me. It would be romantic."

Villicus stared intently at her for a few moments, then smiled wryly and shook his head.

"Come with me now, please."

"What about my shoe?"

They both leaned over, seeing if they could spot it so far below. They could not. They did, however, see Howley's Caddy tearing down Robert's Blvd. at breakneck speed, pursued by over a dozen police cars, all with sirens screaming and lights flashing.

"Oh my God. What's happening down there?"

Trailing above the chase was a police helicopter which was flanked, at a safe distance, by at least five news helicopters.

A block ahead of Howley's car, an officer ran up to the edge of the road and appeared to throw something on the ground.

Howley's Caddy tore over a spike strip that ripped apart three of his tires, sending his car into a spin and then flipping it over. The massive red vehicle skidded along the pavement, shredding the canvas top, and surely shredding the driver, too.

The car came to a stop, pushed partway up onto a sidewalk. Police approached cautiously, their guns drawn. One officer got a bit closer and knelt down to peer in through a side window. Howley burst through the glass and ripped the man's head clean off.

Having killed the officer instantly, wrapped up in the intensity of fighting for his survival, Howley tore into two other officers, not even slowing down from the impact of their bullets. He left their lifeless bodies next to the headless one, then turned and sprinted towards Villicus's building.

"What's he doing?" Amanda cried out, not believing what she was seeing. "Where is he going…?"

The speed at which Howley ran down the road was mind-boggling. He appeared, to the human eye, as a colorful streak. Distracted by the chase below, Villicus suddenly turned and became aware that the sun was just about to break the horizon line. Some light from it was already pouring down the streets, creeping forward like molten gold.

He grabbed Amanda up by her waist with one arm, and turned to ran with her back inside his condo. Still holding her, he slammed his balled-up fist into a control panel that activated a barrier for his massive bay window. Amanda watched, absolutely incredulous, as the light was blocked from the room.

Villicus finally put her down and ran for his office where he fired up all the security cameras he had around the building. Amanda hit the ground a bit too hard, and her feet skidded out from under her.

"Villicus. What are you doing? What is going on here?"

She got to her feet and frantically kicked off her remaining shoe. Running into Villicus's office, she saw him scrubbing through various camera angles until he found one that showed Howley very clearly. Seeing Amanda was there, he slammed the door shut closing them both in and then turned to watch the events unfolding out on the streets below.

Howley made it to Villicus's building but was unable to gain entrance through the locked security doors. Police continued to fire at him. He leapt towards a corner of the building and climbed effortlessly towards the top. Right about the fifth floor, the sun broke the horizon. A building next to Villicus's shielded Howley until he hit the eighth floor, and the rays hit him directly. Howley tried to scramble around to the shadow side of the building; however, he was too late.

His body burst into flames, like an incendiary bomb had hit him. Howley, a writhing, struggling ball of fire, fell away from the side of the building and dropped to earth next to Amanda's shoe. He hit the ground so hard, the flames were extinguished; however, they had done their damage. Howley was destroyed and his body reduced to a pile of smoldering ash that quickly burned itself out.

"*No!*" Villicus cried out when he saw the smoking heap on his monitor.

Police surrounded it, guns drawn.

"What was that? What happened?" Amanda shouted as she moved closer to the monitor, trying to figure what she was looking at.

Villicus pushed her back.

"Talk to me," she shouted at him. "What happened out there? What was that?"

"A friend of mine."

"That was a man that died out there like that?"

"No."

"What was it?"

"He was...like me."

Amanda backed away from him and out into the living room of his condo. Villicus followed her, his gaze fixed and terrifying. The room was dark now. The neon sun sculpture, apparently on a timer, shut off. The only light was from the toys scattered about the room. The colorful lights and carnival like music bounced around the room, creating a surreal effect. The effect was making Amanda even more afraid. What kind of lunacy had she found herself enmeshed in?

Without taking his eyes from her face, he reached over to one of the side walls where the alarm system was. He keyed in a command, and Amanda could hear the solid sound of the door locks engaging.

"Villicus you're scaring me. Let me out of here."

"*No!*" Villicus roared like an animal, causing the glass containers around some of his toys to shatter.

Amanda, watching the terrifying transformation into his vampire self, fell down to her knees. Villicus rushed towards her, hands outstretched, and she cowered before him. Enraged, Villicus turned away and rampaged throughout his penthouse, smashing furniture, toys and his electronic gizmos. He grabbed the motorcycle up and hurled it into the air where it embedded itself in the wall up near the ceiling.

Villicus rushed towards her again. Amanda screamed and covered her face with her hands, so sure she was that her death was imminent. She kept thinking, over and over again, that he would kill her. That he was a killer and would always be one. She didn't know where the thoughts were coming from, but after what she had just witnessed, she felt like it was true.

He was a killer.

He stopped in front of her, towering over her. Cautiously, terrified, she peeked through her fingers up at him. His body shuddered from rage, and his unblinking blackened eyes fixed on her.

Vampire fast, he turned away from her and entered the room where he rested, slamming and locking the door behind him. Amanda could hear him howling in there like a caged, raging beast.

Chapter Twenty-Seven

At casa Bale, the two vampires sat in the dark in the entertainment room, watching over and over again a recording of Howley's death from a local news feed. Each time they saw Howley burst into flames and then fall, they both howled with laughter.

"Do you think Villicus knows?" Nikonar asked.

"Oh, I know he does."

Bale smiled, then shut the recording off.

"You know," he added, "I could just watch that for centuries!"

Both vampires laughed again. Howley had been a thorn in Bale's side for a long, long time. However, Nikonar never knew why. He assumed, at some point, he would hear the sordid tale. For now though, he was happy to bask in the glow of happiness that his master was exuding. It made life, actually his death, much more livable.

Across town, at the precinct where Kim and James were stationed, they too were watching a recording of Howley's demise. Their captain walked into the room where they had been watching and shut the recording off.

"Forensics is still at the scene," he told them, "scraping up what they can. Not a whole lot left. Fire department's helping them, seeing if they can identify the accelerant he might have used. My guess, gasoline. Guy just didn't want to get caught."

Doing his best not to sound like a wise-ass, James asked him, "You think he committed suicide by climbing up the side of a building and then lighting himself on fire?"

"Maybe. Let's just say, I've seen plenty of weird shit in my day and until the fat lady sings on this one, we don't make any assumptions."

"Got it."

Kim had been studying a computer printout. She looked hopeful, then said, "Hey, didn't our tail the other night, the one that followed this Howley Bennett character down to TJ tell us Bennett went with someone, a friend of his?"

"Yes," James said to her.

"And the name of the friend?" she asked.

James picked up a report from the table, near the video playback system, and scanned it quickly.

"Villicus Shanks. That was his building where this guy went whoosh."

"Did you check him out?" Kim asked.

"Yup, nothing."

"Not even a parking ticket."

"Exactly. Just like Ted Bundy."

Kin handed the piece of paper she had been studying and pointed to a name on the list.

"What's this?"

"The friend, Mr. Shanks. He had purchased a large amount of clothing from Henry Bleak's shop on Rodeo Driver and had them delivered to his penthouse, that same address of course… including, a dozen hand-hemmed linen handkerchiefs."

"The same kind from the murder over in Santa Monica?"

"The same."

"Did you try to talk to this joker?" their captain asked.

"We've been calling all morning," James went on, "but no one seems to be at home."

"Time for a search warrant, don't you think captain?" Kim asked.

"It will be really iffy if a judge grants that, but after someone went up in flames halfway up the side of the building, I think I might be able to swing it."

"Thank you, Captain. Okay, James, what do you think?"

"Let's go," James responded, letting a smile cross his lips. "Finally, some action other than gathering up dead bodies."

Kim just shook her head, making sure she had her gun

along with extra ammo, and followed him out the door.

By early evening, they had the warrant in place and had met with the head of SWAT to present their unusual case. Together, they reviewed the possible hazards of paying a visit to Mr. Shanks.

Based on the extraordinary abilities they had seen Howley display, they did not want to take any chances. SWAT was the best they had for this sort of thing, whatever this sort of thing turned out to be.

Inside Villicus's penthouse, Amanda was still trapped. The doors had intricate, well-built locks that she had spent hours trying to break; however, Villicus had them designed to keep prying humans and vampires out. She had found instead a small, heavy sculpture that she was using to try and break the hinges. It was tough going in a room that was predominantly dark.

The huge barrier across the bay window was still in place, blocking any light, and most of the toys and electronic gadgets lay in splinters after Villicus's rampage from the night before. Her only indication that she was even hitting the hinge in the dark was the occasional sparks that would fly up when the sculpture made contact.

She sensed that someone was watching her and turned abruptly, suddenly aware that Villicus was crouched down behind her, just inches away. Panicked, she tried to back away but bumped into the locked doors.

"I won't hurt you, Amanda," he said calmly.

"I don't believe you!" she stuttered through her teeth, chattering from fear. "I know you. I know! You are a killer! You want to kill me!"

"Please trust me."

"Give me one reason."

He knelt and reached for her, but she banged herself into the wall, attempting to elude his grasp.

"I love you. I know that now."

"Don't touch me!"

He paused, observing her in the dark, able to see so much

more than she could. Her eyes remained downcast with tears on her face. Her terror was palpable. In her hands was the small sculpture, and she gripped it tightly.

He went on, "You know what I am, don't you?"

"I think so."

She wanted to scream at him, that she knew he was a killer and would always be a killer, but couldn't put her voice to the words. They felt so foreign and odd to her. *Where were these thoughts coming from?*

"I want you to join me, Amanda."

"What?"

His statement rattled her. She did not know why she thought he meant to kill her, but whatever the reason that intense, alien thought in her mind was dissolving.

"We can be together forever, leave this place behind. Please say yes, Amanda. Please stay with me."

Stepping back, she looked up into his eyes, and saw honesty there. She believed his desire for her to be with him was very real but the fearful things she had seen and experienced with him were affecting her decision. He had shown her his vampire side and the violent, madness that overtook him when he was prepared to kill.

Amanda finally realized, very clearly, that she was not and could not be such a mindless killer. She couldn't accept that. If she became like him, she would be forced night after night for eternity to submit to the hideous bloodlust of what it meant to be a vampire. All of the trappings – the money, and power - were not compensation enough for what she would need to give up.

Maybe, accepting that existence would change her, causing her to actually love it and crave the blood and killing, but that thought, of the glittering monster she would become, froze her with fear and revulsion.

"No," she said.

Villicus felt defeated and completely empty. He backed away from her and went to the bay window, where he opened the barrier across it. He stood there, looking out over the lights of the city silently. After a few moments, Amanda got to her feet and made her way over to stand next to him. The incredible fear she felt for him was dissipating. He looked to her like one of those sad faced little kitties in the cards he would send to her.

"Villicus, I'm sorry, but this life you have, this...existence..., is too costly."

"If you won't join me, then help me, Amanda. You're the only one I trust."

"What do you want me to do?"

"Come with me."

Villicus went back into his office and snapped some of the monitors off the wall. He located a heavy chain in back used to help anchor them during an earthquake. He unraveled the chain and located a padlock and key in a desk drawer, which he handed to her.

Confused, she said to him, "Villicus please talk to me. What are you doing?"

"You were right. This existence comes at too high a price. I had no right to ask you to join me."

"I think I understand why you did."

"I don't want to go on."

"But we can keep what we started, can't we? Can't we!"

"I fear I may eventually kill you. I want it to end. I want this existence I have to end, but I need your help. I can't do this alone."

There was that message again, about him being a killer, but this time, it was coming from him.

"You're going to kill yourself?"

"I'm already dead. Please, Amanda, help set me free."

Crying now, she tugged on the chain he held in his hand.

"This will stop you?"

"It will slow me down, just enough, when the sun comes. Go back inside. Keep far away from me after you place the locks. I will give you the code for all the doors."

He pointed to the door leading to his office.

"You can watch me from in there if you like."

The two of them headed up to the roof and sat on the edge of the building; however, this time, Villicus willingly wrapped his arms around her and held her tight. Together, they waited for dawn.

Across town, at the precinct, James finished strapping on body armor. He was surrounded by several members of the SWAT team. Kim walked quickly into the room.

"Okay, got it. Just going over some last pieces of evidence with the judge. I know I'm late, but I wanted this one by the book."

"No worries," he said to her. "I saved some Kevlar for you."

Outside of Villicus's building, Bale and Nikonar stood out front, aware of the yellow police tape in the corner. Bale looked up towards the roof.

"What are you doing?" Nikonar asked him.

"Just going to finish a few things."

"He was entitled to his revenge."

"He is too dangerous. I should have ripped his heart out when I had the chance."

"You are more surprised than he is that he managed to survive all of that time. I doubt you could have done it."

"Don't be absurd," Bale chided him. "Oh, look..."

Bale indicated with a nod of his head the SWAT team vehicles motoring with purpose towards the building. The two vampires disappeared into the shadows.

"I may not need to do anything at all," Bale snickered.

Nikonar was not so sure.

The SWAT cars pulled up front and Kim exited first, sliding under a section of police tape. She walked to the glass front doors, rapped on them firmly to get the attention of the people at the main desk then slapped her police badge against the glass.

The door was quickly unlocked and Kim, along with James and fifteen SWAT team members, filed rapidly into the lobby.

On the rooftop, Villicus held Amanda and tilted his head back so he could watch the heavens spin above. A slight tinge of pink showed on the horizon, and Amanda felt his body stiffen.

"It's time," he said.

"No, not yet. Just a little longer, Villicus, please."

Gently, he pushed her onto the roof, away from the ledge,

and held the chain out for her. Reluctantly, Amanda took it from him. He rose and walked to a thick metal pipe that was attached to one of the massive vent systems for the building.

Villicus sat down and placed his arms behind his back and around the pipe.

"I don't think you are a murderer, not by choice. Not anymore," she stammered, "I think that if given a chance Villicus, you could leave this..."

"No! No. If you don't do this, then, tonight, I will kill again and I fear, it might be you."

Amanda stood there with the heavy chain dangling from her hands. She realized that nothing she could say would sway his decision. His choice was incredible given his opulent, alluring existence and incredibly powerful nature. Realizing the amazing strength he was showing by asking her to help end his existence, all thoughts of him being a killer left her thoughts completely. Those thoughts were replaced with overwhelming sadness that this phenomenal being was going to leave her."

"This is what you want? You are absolutely sure?"

"Yes."

"There is nothing that can be done?"

He shook his head no.

Amanda knelt with the chain, but before she started to wrap it around his wrists, she kissed him. This time, Villicus returned the kiss.

After a few moments, he pushed her away and said, "We don't have much time."

Crying hard now, Amanda finished with the chain, making it as tight as she could, and put the padlock in place. Quickly, she rose and ran away from him, not daring to look back lest she return and free him.

She headed through the door and then activated the lock behind her with the code Villicus had provided her. She heard the massive steel pins sliding into the edges of the doorframe.

Amanda picked her way through the rubble in the penthouse, heading towards his office. As soon as she was inside, she activated the monitors and was able to see him on the roof. Movement from the corner of her eye caught her attention, and on another monitor she saw the SWAT team entering the elevator on the ground floor.

"No, not now!" she cried out.

The monitor that showed Villicus also showed more of the impending sunrise creeping along the edge of the horizon. He appeared somewhat backlit, his head hanging down in total resignation to the fate he had selected. She wondered how long his acquiescence would last.

The police arrived at the top floor and spilled out of the elevator into the elaborate foyer that fronted Villicus's penthouse. Amanda saw on a monitor that one of them was carrying a battering ram. The other officers, in full SWAT gear, had their weapons drawn, all aimed at the front set of doors.

A female detective approached the door and then banged on it, shouting, "Mr. Shanks! This is the police. We know you are in there. Open the door please. We have a warrant!"

Amanda heard them shouting through the doorway. Looking back to the monitor displaying the roof, she could see Villicus starting to struggle, although it appeared as if he was fighting it. With the way he was shaking his head, it looked like he was trying to maintain control and not fight what was happening to him.

The sun was almost up.

From the front doors, Amanda heard a resounding crash and then the unmistakable sound of wood splintering. One of the doors had its frame knocked right out of the wall, leaving a gaping hole through which the detectives and SWAT team rushed into the penthouse.

Amanda crawled under Villicus's desk but was quickly discovered by the SWAT team who dragged her out into the room.

Fighting and angry, Amanda did her best to break free from the officers holding her but was not successful. Maintaining their grip on her wrists, they deposited her into a chair and held her there.

"What is your name, dear?" Kim asked.

Kim was doing her best to sound professional but also wanted to hurry all of this along. Something seriously weird was going on, but more than that, she sensed that they were close to figuring out who was responsible for the odd, horrifying deaths they had been investigating.

She showed Amanda her badge, and James followed suit.

"I'm Detective Barnstall, and this is Detective Montgomery. You can call me Kim."

"And I'm James," he said as affably as he could, under the circumstances.

Amanda studied the police badges and was doing her best to break the tight hold the SWAT officers had on her.

Kim waved at them to let her go.

Once released, she rubbed her red wrists, then told them her name was Amanda.

"Where is he?" James asked.

"Who?"

"Don't be a fool, Amanda," Kim said.

Her patience was wearing thin.

"Villicus Shanks! Where is he?"

Amanda did her best to keep their attention on her and not on the monitors.

"I, hmmm, gosh, I just am not sure. I really don't know. He left a couple of hours ago. I am sure he will be back soon though."

Kim and James stared down at Amanda, already annoyed with her.

One of the SWAT officers came over to them and pointed through the office doorway at the monitors showing the roof of the building.

"There, look there!"

Amanda could have bitten his arm; however, decided not to.

James and Kim spun around, looking at the monitor.

"What the hell is this?" James shouted.

Kim turned back to face Amanda.

"Where is he?"

"I don't know."

"Where is he!?"

"That looks like the roof," one of the SWAT members said.

"Okay, go...go, go, go!" James shouted.

Kim walked around behind Amanda and put handcuffs on her. She waved the officers away while she kept a tight grip on her elbow.

"We're going to find your boyfriend," Kim told her matter-of-factly.

"Yes, well, maybe that's not such a good idea right now," Amanda said, her gaze firmly fixed on the floor.

She only hoped she had bought Villicus enough time. Amanda and Kim watched the monitor together and saw the door to the roof explode outward as the SWAT team used the battering ram again.

The officers rushed onto the roof, fanning out around Villicus with their weapons drawn. He was fully transformed and in a rage, quickly snapping one side of the chains. His right arm was free while the other was still tangled. Two officers rushed to pin his arm and handcuff him. Villicus grabbed them both up and lobbed them over the side.

Bale and Nikonar saw the two bodies hit the ground below, their limbs snapping and bones disintegrating from the impact.

"Ah, Villicus. That's my boy! Won't go down without a fight," Bale cheered.

Nikonar pushed further back into the shadow and stared at his maker with disdain.

On the roof, Villicus easily snapped the rest of the chain, freeing his other arm and charging back inside the penthouse. His back was smoking where the rising sun had hit him, but he made it back inside, just in time.

He ran to his office and shoved Kim out of the way, slamming her hard into a far wall. She went down, stunned, but still alive.

Villicus advanced on Amanda, sitting in a chair, completely helpless with her hands cuffed behind her back. He grabbed her hair and yanked her head back, ready to take what he had so politely asked for before but had been refused.

"Villicus, please don't!" she begged.

For a brief second, she saw his eyes revert back, but quickly, they turned black again.

Villicus released her just as Kim managed to fire her weapon at him. The shot went wild, and Villicus easily intercepted the bullet that would have hit Amanda. The police, along with James who survived Villicus's attack on the roof, flooded back inside after him.

"Give it up, Shanks!" James shouted.

"I think he went back in here," one of the officers called out.

"Where's Kim? Kim! Where are you?" James called for her.

Villicus burst through the door of his office and raced, vampire quick, to the elevator. He was not interested in riding the car down. Instead, he punched a hole through the floor and raced down the shaft as only a vampire could.

Down below, the workers in the lobby scattered in terror as he burst through the closed elevator doors. The police who had been covering the exits saw him coming and opened fire; however, their bullets did nothing except make a lot of noise. He rushed past them onto the street, bullets hitting him from all sides.

Kim helped Amanda to her feet just as James and the others got to them. As a group, they all move towards the elevator.

Stepping inside, one of the officers nearly fell through the hole, but James crowded them all inside anyway, gripping the sides of the car. Both he and Kim held Amanda by the elbows, facing her towards one of the walls.

The shaft had some lights in it that weren't terribly bright, but they cast enough light to reveal the dizzying distance to the bottom. Amanda turned her face to the wall, fearful of falling to her death and not having any way to hold on to the railings because she still had the handcuffs on.

"Is this thing going to work?" James asked Kim.

She looked at the keypad and hesitated for a second before pressing the "L" key for the lobby.

"Let's hope so," she said.

She used a handheld radio to communicate with the officers outside. The car descended, jerking back and forth, but it was going down at a relatively normal rate of speed. James, seeing how vulnerable Amanda was, looped his arm through hers and held her tightly against the wall.

"This is Detective Barnstall," Kim said into her radio. "I'm coming down with a prisoner. Please advise me of the situation outside."

A voice, crackling through the unit, responded back to her.

"We have the suspect in sight down here. He is running away from the building. We have tried to stop him several times, but he must have some sort of body armor on. Our bullets aren't even slowing him down."

Amanda laughed out loud.

James squeezed her elbow and gave it a firm shake, indicating she needed to quiet down. Amanda just shook her head ruefully and kept her mouth shut.

Villicus flew through the streets, still trailing a piece of chain from his upper arm. He rushed along, staying in the shadows and avoiding the creep of golden light that seemed to seek him out.

He took refuge in a doorway.

Villicus watched people running away, some screaming, as they saw the SWAT teams flood the area. A helicopter circled overhead, advising people to stay indoors and keep the area clear. He saw some officers closing in on him, but even worse than that, he was now cornered by the sun.

A car pulled up nearby, well within his sight, and he saw Amanda, still handcuffed, sitting in the back of the car. He also saw Bale and Nikonar on the other side of the street from him, nearer to Amanda, slinking silently and effortlessly through the shadows. Their movements and presence went unnoticed by the humans in the area but caused him concern over what the hell they were doing.

All focus was on him, so their presence went unnoticed.

Kim moved to the center of the street and, with a small bullhorn, talked to him. She introduced herself and James, then took a couple of steps towards him.

"Mr. Shanks! Villicus! We have your girlfriend with us. We only want to talk with you. Come out with your hands up. We just want to talk."

Villicus crouched down even further in the doorway and

ignored Kim, keeping a watchful eye on the spike of light that grew every closer towards him. The sliver of light might as well have been a well-honed blade, ready to slice into whatever it came across. That one shard could be the end of him.

With his elbow, he punched a hole through the door, only to discover a brick wall on the other side that would take him some time to punch through. He was completely trapped.

Bale, immensely pleased at Villicus's predicament, fully enjoyed the show.

"Observe," he said to Nikonar.

He moved so fast that only Villicus and Nikonar could see him. Bale planted himself under the police car and, with one swift, violent movement, ripped out the floorboard. Amanda stared in horror at his grinning, soulless face looking up at her. His black eyes bore into her.

"No!" Amanda screamed. "Someone, help me!"

Bale grabbed her and ran back, vampire quick, to Nikonar's side in the shadows.

Villicus stared helplessly at her.

"Mr. Shanks!" Kim yelled again. "I am giving you one minute to come out or we come in and get you!"

Bale hugged Amanda closely, leaving her hands cuffed behind her back as he stroked her neck, taunting Villicus.

"No God! Don't let this happen." Bale heard Villicus whisper from across the intersection some eighty feet away.

"My, my, Miss Brax, you are drop dead gorgeous. I'm so glad we finally have had a chance to meet. I think I'll be glad to say that…centuries from now. I did, just so you know, enjoy getting to know your assistant too. Hmmm, what was his name? Oh, that's right, Paul Peter."

Amanda had been staring into his deadly black eyes and felt herself swimming into them, falling for the power he could exude over humans. At the mention of Paul Peter's name, she pulled away from him, letting the grief and anger she felt over his death remove her from Bale's grip on her.

Laughing, he squeezed her tighter, feeling her struggle to breathe. He grabbed her face, painfully, and wrenched it up and around to look back into his eyes. She disappeared again, lost in the blackness of his eyes. The pain she felt over Paul Peter's death was not enough to save her from falling under Bale's control again.

"Bale...wait," Nikonar said to him.

"You will help me, Nikonar," he ordered him.

Bale snapped Amanda's handcuffs apart. Villicus, desperate to help her, called out to Nikonar.

"Nikonar, don't do this. She doesn't want it. We all had the choice. We took it gladly and see where it has brought us."

Bale pulled Amanda's head back so Nikonar could strike.

"Do it...do it now!" Bale shouted at him.

Willingly, she strained to pull her head back even further, so far was she under Bale's influence.

Nikonar started towards her but instead pulled her from Bale's grasp. Startled, Bale fell backwards. Nikonar, in a full rage, completely transformed into his vampire self and rushed forward, pushing Bale into the direct sunlight.

"No..no!" Amanda screamed and tried to follow after him.

The big Russian placed one hand over her eyes and held her closely to his body until the hypnotic grasp Bale had over her passed.

"Don't follow him. Don't look at him." Nikonar whispered into her ear.

The police were startled to see Bale flung into their midst. He fell to the ground and covered his head with his arms, trying to crawl back into the shadows, but parts of him were already igniting.

He could not get back to the shadows in time, and a few officers who rushed towards him, thinking they were helping a man on fire, also went up in flames. The other officers, including Kim and James, backed away in shock.

Amanda, the broken cuffs still on her wrists, pulled free from Nikonar and staggered out into the street. She approached the entrance to the doorway where Villicus hid. He watched her closely, like a cornered animal.

"I don't think I can do this, Villicus," she said sadly. "I don't want to be without you but, I can't do this. I can't be this."

Villicus shook his head furiously and pushed further back into the doorway. From this lower angle, he spied a possible way to escape up between two buildings that were still in shadow. He needed more than anything right now to escape the probing sunlight that sought to immolate him.

To escape though, he knew he would need to leave Amanda in the world she already lived in.

"I want it. I want that...existence. I want you. Please, don't leave me," she pleaded.

"No! You don't want this. Trust me, this is hell. You don't want it."

She took a step closer, where she could almost touch him. Amanda reached out for him, the cuff dangling from her wrist glinted in the powerful sunlight.

She pointed back at Nikonar, who watched them from the shadows.

"I'll do whatever I have to, to follow you. We belong together."

"No, I cannot allow that."

Villicus rose to his full height, took one step forward into the broad swathe of sunlight cutting across the entrance of the doorway and held his hand toward her. Just as their fingers touched, the back of his hand began to smoke. He cried out in pain but took another step toward her and stepped into her arms. She held him tightly, letting the smoke envelope them both, but the sun seemed to darken for just a moment.

Villicus's skin appeared to transform, from its pearly hue to a normal human skin tone. His fangs retreated, and his blackened eyes changed to human ones. Villicus and Amanda clung to each other and waited as the police closed in on them.

He looked up, over Amanda's head, and saw Nikonar hiding in the shadows like a wounded animal. The look on his face was a mixture of shock, jealousy and awe. He roared loudly, causing the windows in the area to shatter, and attracted the attention of the police. His actions gave Villicus and Amanda a few seconds, just enough time, to get away.

Amanda and Villicus ran, racing down through an alley, and avoided detection as the police chased after Nikonar, who disappeared into the shadows.

Kim and James, exhausted from having been up for so long, and at the same time mesmerized by all of the seriously odd things they had witnessed, just stood there, haggard, and worn.

What happened here? What on earth had they just experienced? Where in the hell did their suspects go? What in God's name was that pile of ash on the ground?

They both stared at the pile, not saying a word. What could you say, after seeing a man burst into flame and then turn into… that?

Kim took a few steps back and turned to look down the alley where Villicus and Amanda ran. A few of the SWAT officers were heading back their way, shrugging their shoulders. They had lost the suspect.

What the hell else can happen? James thought.

Standing quietly, both of his hands still cradling his gun, James stared at the pile of ash. A slight breeze had started up. It felt good on his face and neck. Briefly, he closed his tired eyes, then snapped them open again. Something…something was not right.

He looked down at the pile of ash, and saw the surface being tossed about by the breeze that had started up. The gust increased in intensity, and he watched as the surface of the ash started to dance around. Part of him knew he should get something to preserve the pile, to prevent the wind from damaging the evidence. Part of him, though, just did not want to move.

The gust turned into a strong wind that focused only on the ash. He watched in amazement as all of it was whipped into a tightly organized whirlwind that rose up and up then disappeared out of sight.

Epilogue

Along the south of France, by the sea, Villicus and Amanda had made their home.

Villicus wandered the gardens in the soft yellow sunlight, tending roses and breathing in the warm salty air. Amanda, laying comfortably on a wicker recliner rubbed her hand over her swollen belly and watched him wander by the sea as if he had always belonged there. She figured that their child would arrive soon and both of them waited impatiently.

She gently caressed the diamond still hanging around her neck and watched as he walked towards her.

He stepped up onto the beautiful patio, covered by an exquisite trellis adorned with bougainvillea and sweet-smelling vines. The gorgeous golden sunshine created a mesmerizing pattern of shadows across the tile floor weaving slowly about as a light breeze from the ocean gently buffeted the blooms.

Quickly, he leaned over and kissed her, giving her tummy a gentle pat. He sat down in a chair next to her. His phone, sitting on a nearby table, rang.

He answered it, turning on the speaker so they both could listen, assuming it was her doctor calling with a more exact delivery date for their baby. To their surprise though, it wasn't.

Nikonar's plaintive voice drifted out of the phone.

"Villicus... are you there?"

About the Author

"Write what you know" is the classic advice given to authors. Briar Lee Mitchell definitely seems to adhere to that maxim.

The polar setting for Briar's WALKING ON MARS serial echoes her experiences in the world's coldest climate as a guest at McMurdo Base in Antarctica. James Cameron, the producer/director of Titanic traveled with her.

Warming up on Andros Island in the Bahamas helped her set the scene for DARK LIGHTS. She and her dive partners were offered $100 rewards from the Navy base there (AUTEC) should any of them find a live torpedo out in the reefs.

The BIG ASS SHARK author recently donned a wet suit to climb into a shark cage in the northern Pacific. Then Briar and her stalwart search and rescue dog, Thor, patrolled the Georgia woods and succeeded in helping the police locate and recover a missing person. The experience will no doubt fuel her future fiction.

When not engaging in her edgier pastimes, Briar creates paintings for a diverse list of clients ranging from Warner Bros. to the US Air Force. Her work has been featured in films, video games, books, TV and exhibited at the Smithsonian Institution in Washington, D.C. A painting she created after her time spent at McMurdo hangs there or in the Pentagon when it is not on tour with the National Geographic in their traveling exhibit about the South Pole.

She also spends a lot of time floating in her Florida pool watching clouds drift by and imagining mayhem.

Curious about other Crossroad Press books?
Stop by our site:
http://store.crossroadpress.com
We offer quality writing
in digital, audio, and print formats.